I0817967

FOUND YOU

(A Rylie Wolf FBI Suspense Thriller —Book 1)

Molly Black

Molly Black

Debut author Molly Black is author of the MAYA GRAY FBI suspense thriller series, comprising six books (and counting); and the RYLIE WOLF FBI suspense thriller series, comprising three books (and counting).

An avid reader and lifelong fan of the mystery and thriller genres, Molly loves to hear from you, so please feel free to visit www.mollyblackauthor.com to learn more and stay in touch.

ISBN: 978-1-0943-9356-8

BOOKS BY MOLLY BLACK

MAYA GRAY MYSTERY SERIES
GIRL ONE: MURDER (Book #1)
GIRL TWO: TAKEN (Book #2)
GIRL THREE: TRAPPED (Book #3)
GIRL FOUR: LURED (Book #4)
GIRL FIVE: BOUND (Book #5)
GIRL SIX: FORSAKEN (Book #6)

RYLIE WOLF FBI SUSPENSE THRILLER
FOUND YOU (Book #1)
CAUGHT YOU (Book #2)
SEE YOU (Book #3)

CHAPTER ONE

It all came down to this.

Three months of round-the-clock investigations, thousands of false leads, gallons upon gallons of coffee consumed . . . all of it with the promise of one thing: to bring this mean son of a bitch, a man who'd terrorized an entire community for months, down. Now, it was time to make good on that promise.

Cloaked in darkness, under a non-working streetlight at the corner of a run-down section of town outside of Seattle, Rylie Wolf waited for her target to appear. He'd been in there, in his house, for hours, ever since she'd followed him and his old blue minivan back from his job at Beaver Lake Elementary School.

What was he doing?

Instinctively, she reached into her pocket and pulled out her cell phone, lifting it up and tapping the display. The screen was black, the battery dead.

Of course. She got like that sometimes—so focused on a case that even the most essential acts of daily living escaped her. She'd forgotten to plug her phone into the car charger on the way.

Son of a bitch.

So much for calling for back-up.

Just as she made the decision to move closer so that she could venture a look in the windows, the garage door slowly lumbered up.

From her vantage point, she could just see inside. Nothing concerning, just the back end of the blue van with the Washington license plate.

The ignition coughed and fired, the red taillights switched on, and the car slowly began to pull out.

Then, suddenly, it lurched to a stop.

Rylie squinted, trying to see better in the darkness. The single light in the garage bay illuminated the face of one Edison Blaze in the side-view mirror. He was tough, mean, and ugly, the type of guy you wouldn't want to meet in a dark alley. No clue on why the administration had decided it was a good idea to take him on as janitor at the elementary school.

If Rylie had her way, soon, they'd all be regretting that hire. Very soon. *Clean record, my ass.* Someone had fudged those files, big-time.

She watched as he moved in the darkness. He seemed to be wrestling with something in the back seat.

It was just a flash. No more than that. But for a brief instant, she thought she saw, in silhouette, a tiny hand, pressed up against the side window.

Christopher.

The world spun. Her head rushed in a whirlwind, eyes clouding over, breath quickening. This was it. Fingers wrapped around the useless phone, spreading white at the knuckles. She took one unsteady step forward, her sneaker hitting the dewy, slippery grass of the lawn.

Okay. Okay. Think, Rylie. Be calm about this. You can't afford to make any mistakes.

She touched her left hand to her pocket to make sure her car keys were still there. She glanced at her pick-up, across the street, trying to decide if she should make a break for it, now. It was her private vehicle, so she didn't have a radio in there to call for help, but if she made it there, she could peel out and follow him.

Or . . . she could end it. Right here. Right now.

Meanwhile, still halfway out the garage door, the car's driver-side door opened, and out popped the substantial form of Edison Blaze.

Hiking up his sagging jeans, he went back into the house.

In that moment, she made her decision. Grabbing her Glock, she moved forward, pausing at the back of the van, her gun pointed at the slightly-open inside door from the garage to the house. She peered into the window, but saw nothing beyond the darkened pane.

When he appeared in the doorway, he didn't see her at first, as he must've been blinded by the headlights shining in his face. He was carrying a paper lunch bag. He took a few steps toward her, oblivious.

She pointed her gun at her suspect. "Freeze! FBI."

The man did no such thing. Somehow, she'd known it wouldn't be that easy. Edison Blaze had a long list of arrests, but no convictions. He was used to evading blame.

Not this time. She was determined to make sure of that.

Without hesitation, he jumped into the minivan, and it lurched back again. She dove away, narrowly missing the van's rear bumper as it barreled out under a streetlight, revealing him completely. There was a sheen of sweat on his forehead, a wild look in his eyes. Black hair fanned over his forehead like splayed fingers.

She scrabbled to her feet and headed for her pick-up. Jumping in, she punched the gas, tearing onto the road and giving chase.

It was after midnight, so the roads were empty. A light turned red just as she was approaching it. She paused but did not stop as she sailed through the intersection, spotting Blaze, making a right on Sammamish Pike, headed for Interstate 86, the main drag around these parts. Was that where he was heading? It made sense. If he wanted to get out of town—out of the country— quick, that was the easiest way. Headed west, it went all the way to the Canadian border.

And if so, she knew a shortcut.

It paid to have lived here in the suburbs of Seattle for the past sixteen years. From her research, she'd seen that Blaze was a drifter. He'd been making his way up the western seaboard, from Mexico, to California, to Oregon, to Washington, leaving a path of unsolved child abductions along the way. Rylie had connected Blaze to a man in Mexico, who'd sell kids for top dollar, to bidders who'd use them for a variety of shady things. Now, he'd brought his reign of terror to Washington.

And it ends here, she thought, pressing on the gas and taking SE 28th Street, the street before. *Tonight. Because I know these streets better than you, asshole.*

Wheeling into the darkness, at unsafe speeds, she wrapped her hands around the steering wheel. A thin, wispy fog settled over everything, a light drizzle spritzing the windshield. The headlights illuminated the bodies of unsuspecting insects, right before they were pummeled by the pick-up's front end. She turned up the wipers, leaving a track of their gooey bodies behind, worsening her view. On either side of her, there was nothing but sawgrass and tall trees. In the distance, the line of the interstate was marked by the steady stream of red taillights, edging their way toward the Canadian border.

About a quarter mile before Interstate 86, SE 28th Street would intersect with Sammamish. Straining to see, she noticed the headlights up ahead, careening down Sammamish.

It was the van. It had to be.

The van slowed slightly to make the turn onto the interstate. She surged forward, a terrible, reckless idea lodging itself in her head.

Am I really going to do this? she asked herself. Then she asked another question. *Do I want to get this creep, or not?*

The answer: unequivocally, yes.

At that moment, Edison must've noticed her, because he began to pick up the pace, tires screeching.

Too late.

She slammed the front side of the van with such impact, it threw her forward, as the airbag deployed, throwing her back and sending her spinning. A horn blared, and the bones of her neck cracked as she loosened her grip from the steering wheel and slammed on the brakes, waiting for the car to finish fishtailing.

When it came to a stop, all she saw was the sea of white from the airbag. Shoving it and the screaming agony in her back aside, she groped for the door handle and threw it open, then slipped out from underneath it, her hand still on her pistol.

Across the road, she saw a single headlight, shining on the grassy median. There were dark skid-marks from the tires on the road, leading toward where the gravel was disturbed. Beyond that, deep tire ruts in the mud, leading to the van, which was smoking slightly, still.

Rushing forward, gun drawn, she paused when she got close enough, gauging the situation. Then, she reached out and opened the sliding back door.

Darkness. Her eyes couldn't adjust fast enough. Before she could register what was inside, the tires started to squeal and the van began to take off.

Without thinking, she threw herself inside.

She lost her balance almost instantly, thudding backwards onto the empty floor of the van. The interior was bare, which made sense, if it was his work van. When she grabbed for something to steady herself, her gun was thrown from her hands.

Where. . . she thought, looking around frantically for her weapon. But it was gone. For all she knew, it'd flown out the gaping open door of the van. *Likely. Shit. What do I do now?*

The van jolted again, and she stumbled backward, nearly joining it.

Finally, she braced herself against the side of the van. There were no seats back there, no carpeting. There were various tools, things any janitor would use.

But then she saw the frightened form, huddled behind the driver's seat, tiny hands grasping onto a strap on the back of the seat for dear life. The little boy, Christopher, his mouth gagged, wrists and ankles tied, curled as small as could be behind the seat, as if trying to make himself invisible. The fear in his big eyes was heartbreaking.

She knew it.

She'd just known, from the moment she interviewed that guy in the schoolyard after the disappearance, that she was onto something. He'd been so squirrelly. So *wrong*. After ten years as an agent, she'd grown a nose for bullshit. She'd smelled it a mile away with him.

The sight of the poor kid spurred Rylie to action. The van barreled down the median, swaying this way and that. Edison kept looking over his shoulder as he drove, trying to topple her, a wild look in his eye, as if he was enjoying this.

"Edison Blaze. Stop the car," she shouted.

He chuckled. "I'll stop when I'm dead, bitch. Or when *you* are."

From the look in his eye, she knew he meant it. Frantically, she looked around. A toolbox was rattling around in the back, sliding back and forth with every wild turn of the steering wheel. She glanced out the front windshield and saw that they were heading for a bridge. He could plunge them off the edge with a slight turn of the wheel.

Gasping, the next time it slid toward her, she plunged her hand inside. Wrapping her fingers around a wrench, she dove forward, bringing the full weight of the metal tool down on his temple.

He let out a growl and lost control. The van fishtailed wildly, brakes and tires squealing. She scrambled backwards, grabbing the little boy in her arms and holding him in the cocoon of her body. Just in time, because a split second later, she felt her body shoved end over end, falling, weightless for a moment, before slamming down, hard, on the ground.

And then, mercifully, silence.

Almost immediately, she sprang into action, ignoring the swimming of her vision and the pain in almost every limb. She let go of Christopher, hearing his muffled cries, but it was too dark to see much of anything except the opening to the van, which was now above her, framing the starry sky.

She set him down gently. "Stay here," she whispered. "Let me check things out first."

Bracing herself on the frame, she crawled out, climbed toward the passenger-side front door, and opened it, hoping to see Edison Blaze, knocked out or dead.

But the seat was empty.

There was the sound of swishing grass behind her. Slowly, she turned around to face him.

Her first reaction was a sense of wonder at how big he looked, up close. The pictures never conveyed that. He stood over six feet and broad-shouldered, wearing a black T-shirt stretched over his muscular frame and dirty blue jeans. Blood trickled down his temple and the sneer on his face said that he wasn't happy with her intrusion. .

"You're Rylie Wolf," he whispered. "Right? Wasn't that what you said your name was? FBI. You're the one who has been on my tail, all this time."

Her mouth worked, lips spreading, but no sound came out. She couldn't even think of what to say.

She took a single step toward him, a thousand thoughts flying through her mind as he coiled his legs and charged at her, his mouth twisting into some alien snarl full of teeth. The snarl was all she could see in the dim moonlight before her body was swallowed in an avalanche of muscle, blurred motion, and a strange, guttural growl of hatred and rage. He slammed into her, shoulder drilling into her chest, propelling her clumsily backwards, thudding against the dewy ground.

She felt something sharp dig between her shoulder blades a split second before it exploded and splayed apart on either side of her. The jagged remnants of the small bush, or whatever it was, tore at her shirt and skin under his assault.

Her vision clouded and darkened, the black of endless night creeping in from the edges, forcing a kind of tunnel vision. He was everything she saw, pushing forward, arms extended, one hand on each shoulder, flanking her collarbone and pressing backwards, straining her every muscle.

"Finally," he growled, his breath sour and rank. Neat rows of forehead wrinkles twisted into strange divots of anger above his narrow, piercing eyes. Crow's feet extended from the edges of each of them, and his wide nose crinkled into a stubbed toe of flesh and cartilage. He had more than a five o'clock shadow spread across his jawline and down his neck.

She closed her eyes as, despite her best efforts to stop him, his hands slid from her shoulders and start to close around her throat, narrow, muscular fingers wrapping all the way around and starting to squeeze.

Frozen. Completely immobile. Pain flared between her shoulders and down the length of her back, but it was nothing compared to the burning in her lungs. His strength was incredible, the pressure undefeatable.

Somewhere, little Christopher began to cry.

Stop it. Stop it, Rylie. That boy needs you.

The assailant's fingers closed tighter, and her breath lessened. All the while, she stared up at him, wondering if this was the last sight she'd ever see, The blue eyes bore deep into hers, and she shook her head, tossing her long, curly hair down over his wrists. His narrow smile exposed yellow teeth, illuminated by the single glowing headlight, and bathed her in horrific breath.

She reached towards his hands in a pleading motion, fingers spread and palms open, trembling for some sort of mercy, but she could tell from the look on his face that he had none. Fingers closed even more tightly, and he pushed back even harder.

She wrapped her fingers around his wrist, and by then, he was so intent on his victim that he didn't even notice.

With her right hand clasped tight, she pulled at his wrist while her left hand came up from her hip and struck underneath the same wrist. Torquing her hips, she tore his wrist up and away, and his fingers released, springing apart like an opening latch.

Using the full momentum of her body, she rolled her shoulders and tangled his arms together, then spun, propelling herself off the ground and ramming her hip into his waist. His feet left the floor, and he was carried over her hip into a clumsy forward roll, his shoulder slamming against the ground. Frantically, she backpedaled as he came to a stand, face enraged, and charged again, barreling into her with his right shoulder. She toppled backwards.

"Bitch!" he bellowed and lunged at her, wrapping his huge hands around her shoulders and lifting her off the ground. "I'm going to kill you!"

He meant every word of it, she knew, even before he spun and sent her sideways through the air until she slammed into the cold, wet ground. Sparks blasted behind her eyes. He advanced again, but the moment she hit the floor, she bounced up in a mad scramble. Every muscle in her body screamed, and she could barely catch her breath. Even so, she had to. Getting into ready position, she prepared for the attack.

Then she heard the sound of sirens.

Edison Blaze must've heard them, too, because he suddenly dropped his hands, which were raised to wrap around her throat. He straightened for a moment, listening, and then said, "Shit."

He broke into a run.

Ignoring the pain screaming through every nerve in her body, she pursued him, driving through the long sawgrass. Much of the time, she couldn't see him. She had to stop to listen for him, and only once in a while, she'd see his large body, moving up ahead. He climbed to the asphalt surface of the road and started to run for the bridge, but when he got to it and peered over, he stopped and turned around. A police car skidded to a stop, and two officers emerged, guns drawn. "Freeze!" one said.

He staggered forward, as if on his last legs, and lunged for escape. When more police joined the fight, he spun around, helpless. Seeing nowhere to go, he held up his hands in surrender.

Breathing hard, she finally allowed her body to relax. One of the officers turned to her, gun drawn. "Agent Wolf? Is that you?"

She nodded, still unable to speak, her lungs burning. She clutched the knot in her side. Her daily five-mile run hadn't been enough to prepare her for *this*—hot pursuit after nearly having all the air strangled out of her by a man twice her size.

"I've done nothing wrong," Edison Blaze whined as they approached him.

Sure, you haven't, Rylie thought as she turned and headed back toward the van. By now, Christopher's cries had become steady, mournful sobs. She climbed inside the open door and looked at the little boy. Other than a few scrapes and bruises that most normal seven-year-old boys had, he seemed okay. She smiled. "Hey, you. Is your name Christopher?"

He nodded, fear in his face.

"I'm Rylie Wolf from the FBI. I'm here to get you home. You want to go home?"

He stared at her for a long time. Then he said, "Y-you have a badge?"

She pulled it out from the pocket of her jacket, and showed it to him. "Want to hold onto it for now?"

He nodded and took it, staring at it with awe. "I want my Mom."

She motioned him forward, and he allowed her to scoop him into her arms, then clung on for dear life. "And I promise you. She wants you, too. So let's get you back there, okay?"

Her body aching, she carried him toward the closest cop car, seeing double. She already knew she was going to catch hell from Matthews for this, but she didn't care. That was tomorrow. No matter what, it would be worth it.

CHAPTER TWO

Calvin McCrea hated vacations.

While most of the world counted off the days until their escape to paradise, Calvin looked forward to their annual drive to their getaway on the Gulf Coast with a mix of dread and apprehension.

All because of her.

His loving wife of thirty-four years, Darla, was a wonderful woman in all respects, but when it came time for them to use their Naples timeshare, she morphed into a different woman. She planned every outing to the second, marking off different points of interest they could visit along the way that would be both new and educational. She started packing *months* before. She even insisted on having boatloads of sunscreen for the week, as if the state of Florida didn't sell sunscreen. It was like this, every year. "I just don't want anything to go wrong!" she'd say, all the while, mapping out what route they needed to take, to the mile.

And she was only getting worse. She played the what-if game constantly in her head, so that now, their annual vacation was officially more trouble than it was worth.

Two days' worth of travel. Forty-three hours, to be exact, not counting stops. Not for the first time, Calvin stretched his sore back, adjusted his numb backside on the seat, and wondered why they'd gone and fallen in love with the Gulf Coast. It was just too damn far away.

"That pile-up back there in Missoula cost us over two hours!" Darla moaned from the front passenger seat of their Buick. "This is awful."

"Now, now, dearest. It would only be awful if we were in it," he reminded her, trying to be jovial. Once they got there, once he started fishing with a beer in his hand, things would be better. He hoped. Fishing off his old boat was one of the few joys he had left in life. "You got to see that Elmer's Fountain, right? Knock that one off the ol' bucket list."

She nodded. "I know. It was interesting, wasn't it? I'd always wanted to stop. It's just—that dust-up with that trucker back there at the

Dairy Freeze Service Center really scared me. I told you, you shouldn't go talking to anyone you don't know at these roadside places."

He gritted his teeth. Not his finest hour. The trucker—a guy from Idaho, from his license plate—had gotten all in Cal's face. He'd just wanted to tell him he admired his cab. It was a nice one—all tricked out with a real nice custom paint-job. Cal, an automotive guy himself, appreciated such things. But the guy had jumped down his throat. For a second, he'd been afraid the man was going to pull a gun. After that, they'd backed off and jetted out of there, fast. "Well. We got gas. We should be good for a while."

"But we're not going to get to the hotel outside of Ranchester on time," Darla complained, staring at the GPS on her phone.

"What? Do you think they'll close? We have a reservation."

She gnawed on a fingernail. "Yes, but it's three hours away. And I'm still bitter that we missed that Garden of One Thousand Buddhas."

"Ah, there'll be other times, love."

"I know." She said it like she didn't believe it. "But it's so late."

He took her hand and held it. "I'm fine to drive."

"I don't know about that," she said, studying him.

Truthfully, he was feeling a little ragged around the edges. It was after nine, and at home, by this time, he'd be in his recliner, dozing off. Add to that the harrowing six-hour drive from where they'd stopped last, off Route 86 in Superior, and his nerves were just about shot.

But they had to make it to the Holiday Inn Express on the Montana-Wyoming line. That was where Darla had booked them. And she'd spent hours, pouring over reviews to find a place that was clean, bed-bug free, comfortable, and had a suitable complimentary breakfast that wouldn't upset his dairy allergy.

As much as he tried to stifle it, just then, a long yawn came out. "Really. No. I'm good."

She reached into the back seat and pulled out her Thermos. "I packed coffee for this, just in case."

"Ah, you think of everything," he said, as she poured him a mug. He brought it to his lips and tasted it, then frowned. "That's pretty awful. It tastes like dish detergent."

"Does it?" She tasted it and made a face. "Ew."

He laughed.

Darla didn't seem to find it very funny. "Oh, no. I was so busy packing, I probably didn't wash the Thermos out well enough." She spilled the coffee back into the Thermos and tightened the lid. "Oh, nuts. That's a disappointment."

"It's all right. I'll manage."

A moment later, while they were listening to a particularly slow song on the radio, he realized he was drifting off the road when he heard the bump-bump-bump of the uneven pavement. That wasn't good. Maybe he *couldn't* manage. He blinked, then cracked a window, letting the cool air hit his face.

And now, he realized, he had to relieve himself.

This *really* wasn't good. The problem was, this stretch of highway, through the Indian Reservations, had very few exits, all of which had questionable facilities, if they had any at all. Darla rated truck stops and exits for how clean the facilities were. And Calvin specifically remembered her saying there weren't very many in this stretch of Montana, passing straight through the Crow Indian reservation.

He checked the time. They had at least three and a half hours to the state line. No way was he going to make it. He had to stop.

Just then, he spied a sign that said, *ST. XAVIER REST AREA- EASY ON! EASY OFF! OPEN 24HRS! RESTROOMS- VENDING MACHINES! NO GAS! CLEAN!*

He thought he had found the answer to his prayers, so he navigated to the ramp. It led out into nothing but darkness, like a road to nowhere. In fact, all around them, there was nothing but trees. It seemed as though there was nothing else around for miles, which meant it was a good thing they'd come upon it when he had. His bladder strained almost to its breaking point, begging for relief.

"Wait. Where are you going?" Darla asked, gripping the door handle in alarm.

"I have to use the restroom. I had two waters at lunch, remember? And this is as good a spot as any."

She shook her head and paged through her phone. "I don't know about that. This place isn't even on my Travel-wise app."

He chuckled. "Maybe because it's new. I don't remember seeing it last time we were here."

She wrinkled her nose as her eyes volleyed around the place, drinking it in with horror. "I don't know if that's such a good idea. You know what they say about this highway."

He laughed. "That's all superstition. It's not real."

"I don't know about that. Besides, you don't remember the rest stops you don't need to stop at, Cal. And we've never had to stop at someplace like this. It'd got to be some big emergency for me to want to stop here."

He waved her away. "It is an emergency, hon. It's fine. I'll be in and out. You have any change? I'll get myself a Mountain Dew. That'll keep me up."

"You're pre-diabetic. Besides, you want to pee again?"

"I'll get a diet. And I need *somethin'*," he said as they pulled into the parking lot. Sure enough, there was a long line of parking spots, but not a single other vehicle in sight. The lot wasn't very well lit; in fact, there was only a single bulb shining in the entire complex, on the porch between two small stone buildings. One had a MEN sign on the door, the other, a WOMEN sign, though someone—an ardent feminist, likely— had scratched out the E there and put a Y. He spied a few vending machines in the alley between them.

But it seemed clean, and harmless.

He held out a hand to her. "Change?"

She looked down at it. "Are you sure you want to do this?"

"I *have* to do it, dearest. Or I'll wet my pants," he said with a smile.

She dug into her purse and pulled out a dollar bill and a few quarters, pressing them into his palm. "All right."

"You want anything? I can see if they got some of those Little Debbie Honey Buns you like?"

She shook her head. "I've lost my appetite. Just hurry back, okay?"

"You got it. And I hope you have an appetite tonight. I'm taking you out for a late steak dinner." He opened the door and stepped out. Then he turned back to her and tilted his head. "You should at least get out and stretch your legs. You know what the doctor said. All that sitting ain't good for your back. Stretch, baby."

She shook her head stiffly and clutched her purse on her laps with both hands, trembling a little. "I'll just wait here. Go fast, Cal."

He skipped into a jog and hurried to the door to the men's room. When he got there, he waved at his wife. She was sitting there, white-knuckling her purse on her lap, her face pale as the moon. He smiled, but she didn't smile back.

He pushed open the door to the bathroom, thinking about how much farther they'd have to drive. Three and a half hours meant they wouldn't have to stop for gas the next morning until they reached the Black Hills, and maybe they'd make it all the way to the South Dakota state line. Then, they could get gas after breakfast in Rapid City. Darla would be okay with that.

It was dark inside. At first. He swept his hand across the tile wall to find a switch, and finding nothing, muttered a curse. He'd just begun to push the door open and scan the other walls with the scant light from the dim bulb outside, when a light came on.

Motion activated, he thought. *Makes sense. Saves money. I bet this place is empty, most of the time.*

And it was now, he realized, as he walked down the aisle of open doors, his every footstep echoing on the tile.

When his eyes caught on something that shouldn't have been there, the lights went out.

He held his breath, and for a moment, he almost peed himself.

No. My eyes are just seeing things. That was nothing.

He squeezed his prostate and clenched his hands into fists, helpless, listening for some sound. The only thing he heard was the rhythmic dripping of the nearby faucets.

The light went back on just as suddenly as it had gone off. Then, it flickered wildly.

Damn motion-sensing's out of whack. I've got to keep moving, he thought, waving his hands about.

Then he strained to see what he thought he'd seen before, hoping it would prove to be an errant garbage can, or something else.

But no. It was just what he'd thought it was.

A pair of shoes, in the last stall, with too-long gray pants attached. The toes of the black work boots were pointing toward him, as if they belonged to someone who was peering through the crack between the stall doors.

Watching him.

"Hello?" he asked, his voice cracking, but the figure did not respond. It didn't even move.

The lights flickered again. Moving his hands about, they came on. He looked over at the stall, gauging how long it would take to relieve himself. If he did, he'd have to turn his back to this person, and who knew what the person would do?

Taking a deep breath, he walked, slowly, toward the man. "Hello?" he called again, getting back some of his voice.

When he was near the door, he braced himself, and pushed it open.

"*Arugh!*" the man inside screamed, jumping, making Calvin jump just as high.

The man was wearing a headset, playing some kind of lively Mariachi music. Contrary to what it had looked like, he'd been leaning against the back of the stall, holding his mop in his hand and lazily leaning up on it. Now, Cal could see it with clarity—the rolling bucket, the dark uniform. A janitor.

Calvin clutched at his chest as the man, clearly annoyed, spouted off at him in Spanish. He held up his hands in surrender. "I'm sorry. *Lo siento,"* he said, quickly reversing direction when he thought of poor Darla. He'd left her out there, far too long.

He did his business in the stall closest to the door, then washed his hands quickly and went outside, picking the change out of his palm. He fed it into the vending machine, noticing his only choices were Fanta and regular Coca Cola. No diet anything. He'd catch hell from Darla, but in the end, she'd understand—it was better than falling asleep at the wheel.

The bottle falling to the bottom of the machine was the loudest sound for miles as he reached into the door and pulled it out. Grabbing it, he untwisted the cap, took a satisfying swig and jogged back to the lot.

The moment he rounded the corner and saw his pick-up, though, he knew something was wrong.

Darla's face had been so pale with worry, before, that it shone like a beacon. Now, though, he couldn't see it.

He kept moving nearer, thinking that maybe she'd lowered her head to look at her phone, or that she was going through their luggage to make sure they'd packed some other thing that they couldn't possibly get in the state of Florida. But as he neared, he realized the seat was empty.

Standing in front of the car, he looked around. She must've gotten out to stretch her legs, after all.

He scanned the area around the rest stop, and finding nothing, opened the door to the car and looked inside. Her phone was resting in the cup holder, and her purse was open, on the front seat, its contents spilled. An Excedrin bottle rattled noisily on the foot mat.

A tendril of fear crept up Calvin's spine. She wouldn't leave her phone or her purse, no matter where she went, even if it was a short walk to stretch her legs.

"Darla!" he called, but the only answer was the crickets and other evening wildlife.

He reached over the seat and began to pile her items back into her purse. Wallet, keys, a sleeve of gum, his back pills, more tissues than she knew what to do with. When he picked up the last pile, he noticed it.

Dark red droplets, seeping into the camel-colored upholstery of the seat.

He reached over and touched them. Still wet. He brought his fingertips under the overhead light and inspected the tacky substance. Blood.

Fear rising inside, he jumped out of the truck and rushed to the other side, falling to his knees on the asphalt.

His stomach dropped when he noticed more drops of blood, like a trail, leading out into the unknown. He followed them a short distance, to the middle of the road, where they abruptly disappeared.

He let the soda fall to the ground, reached for his phone, and dialed 9-1-1, hoping against hope that he'd have good enough reception along this desolate stretch of interstate.

CHAPTER THREE

The following week, when Rylie Wolf walked into the FBI's Field Office for the Analysis of Violent Crime in Seattle, she already knew she was going to get read the riot act.

It didn't matter that they'd all sent her a giant bouquet in the hospital, wishing her well and hoping she'd be back at work soon. It didn't matter that the media was lauding her as a hero. It didn't matter that Christopher's family and several of her fellow agents had called her, expressing their congratulations on a job well done.

Bill Matthews, the Unit Chief and her boss, was going to rain on her parade.

According to her friends on the force, he was pissed off. But when was he not, over something she'd done? The two of them had never seen eye to eye, from his very first day on the job.

The knowledge hadn't made her recovery easy. Bill Matthews might have gotten the job simply because his father was Deputy Director, but while he'd made his share of mistakes working a job he knew very little about, where Rylie was concerned, he always seemed to pull out the FBI rulebook and turn everything into a grumble-fest.

Right now, she got the feeling that the grumbling was about to land on her.

But she was ready. As she stepped inside, arm still in a sling, waving half-heartedly at the co-workers she hadn't seen in a week, she practiced what she would say. The Thompsons, Christopher's parents, were overjoyed. She had the police force on her side. No one had been hurt. In the eyes of the media, they were golden. So what if her methods were a little unorthodox? They'd gotten their guy. Without her, Edison Blaze would've murdered or pawned off little Christopher into the trafficking rounds, and been free to do the same to how-many-other innocent kids?

No. She was blameless. As she'd told Cooper, who'd called her to clue her in on Matthews's grumblings, it was just a misunderstanding. She'd clear it up.

When she stepped onto the floor of the Behavioral Analysis Unit, the entire place—and it was a wide, busy floor, full of agents and low-walled cubicles as far as the eye could see— burst into applause.

She blushed, hating the attention. She knew she'd done well, and wouldn't have done it any other way, screw Matthews. But she hadn't expected a standing ovation. Especially since most of the people here just tolerated her. Respected her. They didn't exactly qualify as *friends*. She didn't really make those.

"Go get 'em, Killer," Cooper Rich, who had the desk opposite her, said, giving her his million-dollar smile. If she could call anyone a *friend*, it was probably him, but not really. He tugged on her sling. "Your arm okay?"

"Thank you," she said softly, taking the sling off. They'd been borderline flirting, on and off, since they arrived at Quantico. He'd risen in the ranks faster than her, though, probably because he didn't have the temper she had. "It's fine. I don't even need this thing, really."

"Before you get too comfortable," Lisa Fairlane, Matthews's executive assistant said, still clapping for her. "Bill said he wants to see you as soon as you come in."

Rylie looked at her, trying to gauge her expression. From the look on her face, it wasn't anything good. Her eyes went to Bill's corner office. The door was closed, but she could see his chunky silhouette as he leaned back in his chair, feet on the desk. And his voice—he was so loud, she could hear everything he was saying. He was chewing out someone for "embarrassing him," completely oblivious to how much he embarrassed himself, on his own.

Lisa gave her an apologetic look as she put her things on her desk and took the first step toward his office.

This is one way to make a Monday even worse, she thought as she waited outside for him to finish his call. Occasionally, someone on the floor would look up at her, their eyes full of sympathy.

The truth was, the only person in the department who liked Matthews was his dad, and that was because he was Deputy Director.

When she heard him slam the phone down on its cradle, she knocked twice and went inside. "You wanted to see me."

He looked up, a sneer on his puffy face. He was only about a decade older than Rylie, and yet he looked like an old man, with his round belly and receding hairline. His father, at least, was stately and looked good at press conferences. Bill Matthews always looked tired and constipated. “Oh. Wolf. You’re here,” he said tiredly, as if he’d rather her be gone for good.

No wonder he’d failed his bid for state senator. He’d been a genuine screw-up all his life, even after his daddy had put him through Yale Law. He’d gotten into more than a few scandals with women in his office, done a few dirty deals, and then, it’d all come to light right before election day. He’d not only lost; he’d lost *spectacularly*.

And he *still* had the nerve to show his face in public.

Not only that, but his father then had to do something with him. Unfortunately, he’d made him Unit Chief, even though he hadn’t spent a day in Basic Training at Quantico. Even though she wasn’t really sure he knew what FBI stood for.

Rylie had been the only female in her class at Basic Training, and it’d been the hardest thing she had to do. To see a man like Matthews, who chain-smoked and possibly did even worse on his days off, breeze through the doors at Quantico without so much as lifting a finger—well, as her mother used to say, it burned her bacon.

“Yes,” she said, hovering in the doorway. “You had something to tell me?”

He scowled at her like she was an unsightly blot on his carpet. “You know damn well what I wanted to tell you. In case you didn’t know, I’ve been calling you, all week.”

“Yes, I know . . . I was recovering.”

“And you didn’t have time to call your supervisor back?”

She shrugged. “The painkillers . . .”

He waved it away. “Doesn’t matter. You’re here now. So I finally get to ask you. What the hell did you think you were doing out there?”

She crossed her arms. Behind her, you could hear a pin drop. She got the feeling that everyone on the floor was listening, and maybe had been waiting all week, to hear this exchange.

“I think I was capturing a wanted criminal who was a danger to the public, sir,” she said, her voice even.

“No,” he splayed his hands over his belly and leaned back, a satisfied smile on his face. “I think what you were doing was going against the rules. As usual.”

“Possibly. But the main objective was to catch the man, right? And I—”

“Catch the man, yes. Tear up half a mile of highway? The median’s a wreck. They say it’s going to cost millions of dollars to fix!”

She scoffed. “To plant a few bushes? Come on—"

He lunged forward without warning and slammed his palms down on his blotter. "You deliberately disobeyed orders. What about calling for back-up?"

"My phone was dead," she said calmly.

"According to the police report, you slammed your government-issued vehicle into the side of his van."

"That's right. I had to stop him."

"You could've injured the victim!" he shouted at her. Now, she was sure everyone on the floor was listening. "Not to mention that it was another hundred-thousand dollars' worth of equipment you destroyed."

"I didn't mean to. And I wouldn't have hurt the kid. I made sure to hit the *front* of the car—"

"But still, you put that child in danger."

"The Thompsons didn't see it that way. They were grateful to have him back. And he wasn't hurt. Not at all. He's spending his nights home, safe, in bed, instead of in a cage. So it all worked out."

He pointed a fleshy finger at her. "You're *lucky* it all worked out. The next time, you might kill someone, or yourself. You understand me?"

Rylie let out a sigh. "Yes. I understand." *But that doesn't mean I'd have done anything different. If I hadn't done what I did, Christopher might not be alive today.*

He eyed her suspiciously. "I don't think you do. I can't have you endangering others and yourself, destroying property, just on a whim. The FBI handbook exists for a reason."

Right, for you to recite to me every time I do something that takes the spotlight off you. "The handbook is a guideline." At least, that was what Bruce Masterson, the former FBI Unit Chief, used to say, before he retired, last year. She hadn't technically *liked* Bruce—she didn't really like anyone—but they'd gotten along all right.

Matthews, though, was a sad substitute for Masterson. He pounded the desk with a single fist. "It should be your bible! I don't want you doing a single thing unless you find it in the pages of that book. You got it?"

"I've got it," she said mock-pleasantly, trying to keep the lid on the pot inside her, which was threatening to boil over. It had happened so much, she'd come to learn the warning signs. *Breathe. Calm. You lose your temper now, it'll just get worse. It always gets worse when you do.*

His eyes narrowed. "Do you really?"

She fisted her hands on her hips. "What is that supposed to mean?"

He clenched his teeth, his smug, fat lips and punchable face so readily available for her to land a perfect right hook. "Because I seem to remember bringing you in here to discuss this very thing, just last month. And the month before that."

"Yes, but—"

"But nothing, Wolf. Stop being so emotional! If you don't put your female emotions under control and get your act together . . ."

That was it. She could only humor sexist, pretentious blowhards for so long. And her limit had definitely been reached.

She stepped forward and put both hands on his desk, leaning forward as if she was about to whisper something. But instead, she spoke at full volume. "Listen, you pretentious prick. You only got this job because your daddy needed someplace to put you where you'd stay out of trouble. You have no business being here. And you certainly don't have any business telling any of us how to do our jobs."

Then she turned on her heel and stomped out of the room, slamming the door behind her.

The floor burst into even louder applause than before.

Two standing ovations in one morning? So it was a good Monday, after all.

*

There was so much paperwork to catch up on that by the time Rylie got out of the office, it was after nine.

Not that she had anything to go home to.

She took the bus to her apartment building just on the outskirts of Seattle, in Lake Hills. She ran up the stairs to the fifth floor, to get a little exercise in. Then she pushed open the door, grabbed a carton of leftover Thai from the fridge, and sat down to binge-watch terrible reality television.

As she sat there, scarfing down her food, she thought of Bill Matthews. What an awful man. She'd respected her former boss—he was a military hero, a family man, and an all-around good person. But Bill? He was everything Bruce Masterson was not.

Every time she looked up at him, for the rest of the day, he was there, sneering at her. She had the feeling whatever was going on in his head wasn't good. He held grudges. And yes, he had the power to make her life a living hell. Every time she looked at him, she could almost see the fantasy of him, humiliating her, in a cartoon bubble hanging over his head.

Her phone buzzed. She looked over at it. It was a text from Cooper: *Has the pretentious prick said anything else to you?*

She winced. Had she really called Bill, her boss, that? She typed in: *No. Did you think I overdid it?*

Why do you care what I think?

She got the feeling he was just procrastinating. *Because you're a GS-14 Step 6. I'm just a lowly 4.*

It had been a bone of contention for a while. One day, she'd accidentally gotten a look at his paystub and found that despite them being hired at exactly the same time, he'd been promoted twice more than she had been. At first, she'd blamed sexism, but the more she thought about it, the more she realized that he deserved to be her senior agent. He did everything by the book. And she didn't. She had that *temper*. She called her supervisors pretentious pricks. No wonder they liked him better.

His response made her cringe. *Okay, maybe just a little bit.*

Damn. Cooper was always right. She'd never met a straighter arrow, which was why she knew that they would never get along if they dated. Sometimes, she just couldn't control her tongue. It didn't matter how much Bill Matthews deserved it. It didn't matter that everyone thought he was a prick. Some things, you just didn't say to your boss.

She typed in: *I'm in trouble, aren't I?*

His response was: *Guess we'll see.*

That meant she was *definitely* in trouble. Where she was direct, Cooper was big on mincing words. No wonder everyone liked him so much. He had so much tact; he could tell a person to go to hell—not that he ever did— and they'd enjoy the trip.

She stared at the phone, wishing he'd say something else, like, *How about a drink?* or *Want to catch dinner?* But there was nothing else. Ten years together in the FBI, and they'd always danced around the idea of dating. But he'd never pulled the trigger. Sure, she'd had boyfriends, and he'd had girlfriends, so she'd chalked it up to bad timing. But she and Dan had broken up four months ago, and Cooper worked so much she doubted he was seeing anyone anymore, either. So what was the deal?

She thought about asking him, but the truth was, right now, she didn't feel up to dating. And sometimes, his straight-arrow ways were just plain annoying. So maybe it was better if he didn't ask her. He probably didn't want to mix business and pleasure, anyway. And he was likely right about that, too. It could get sticky.

When it was clear the conversation with Cooper was going nowhere, she set her phone aside and looked around her bleak, empty apartment. She'd been living here for ten years, too, and it still wasn't home. In fact, all the personal touches—the artwork, the overstuffed sofa— had been Dan's. She didn't have time to devote to decorating. And she didn't have time for pets, either. So that left her alone, in a dark, cramped apartment with absolutely no character whatsoever.

She hadn't had time for Dan, either.

That's probably why he'd left. After three years together, he'd just cashed in his chips and walked out without so much as a goodbye, lost her phone number, and disappeared off the face of the earth. And she was surprised when he was gone, that she really didn't care very much. He'd kept telling her she was a "hard woman to know," and she guessed that was true. She didn't really want anyone to know her.

She settled into the couch and stared at the television, her eyes feeling heavy. This was probably why she loved reality television. These people were unafraid of laying their souls bare, revealing their secrets to the whole world. It felt like a train wreck to her—a cautionary tale to keep her cards close to her chest.

She blinked, and when she opened her eyes again, she was sitting in the back of the massive RV, on one of the bunks beside the kitchen, watching Rose cook breakfast. The abundant sunshine framed her face, lighting up the flowered wallpaper and making everything bright and happy.

"You hungry, Ry?" Rose said, smiling up at her as she scraped scrambled eggs into a plate. "Sleepy girl. You and Maren and Kiki must've stayed up way past your bedtime!"

She laughed, rubbing her eyes, and looked around. "Where are they?"

Maren was her older sister, Kiki was Rose's daughter. They'd been neighbors in Enumclaw, and fast friends—almost like family. Rylie and Kiki had done everything together, so that was why Rose had invited her and her mom and Maren on a "Girls Trip" in their family RV that summer, tooling about the campsites around Yellowstone. It had been so fun, on the road, like a dream—driving most of the day, hooking up the campsite at night, drinking Cokes and margaritas while they sat by the fire and shared stories.

And then, everything had changed.

The always smiling, cherubic woman with the yellow curls looked to the window, and dropped the pan to the ground with a clatter. Hot oil spattered everywhere.

Suddenly, the clouds rolled in, casting dark shadows over the kitchen. Thunder boomed overhead.

"Rylie," Rose warned, wiping her hands on her apron and heading for the door. "Go to the back bedroom now."

She scampered down from the bunk and froze there. Her parents always told her that the back bedroom was off-limits to kids. "But—"

"Do it! Now!" she shouted in a voice Rylie had never heard her use before.

More thunder boomed, and the earth shook with bright light, as if lightning had struck nearby. It spurred Rylie into action. Her skinny limbs working, she scrambled to the back of the RV and buried herself under the covers.

That was when she heard the rain, pattering against the metal roof of the RV.

She stayed there, though she wasn't sure how long. When the rain began to let up, she pulled herself out from under the covers and went to the door.

The bodies were there—Kiki, Rose, and her mother. They'd all been shot, once, in the head.

But no Maren. Maren was gone.

She'd stood over the bodies of the three females and sobbed her heart out. She had no idea what happened next. It was all a void. The trauma of that moment had been permanently embedded in her mind, so that it was the first thing she saw, every time she closed her eyes.

Rylie blinked awake to find herself on her couch, an empty television screen in front of her. She turned off the television and shuddered.

That day, when she was nine years old, was the most horrible day of her life. She dreamed of it, all the time. But most often, she thought of her older sister, Maren, who'd been twelve. She'd disappeared without a trace. Sometimes, when Rylie thought of her, out there, she imagined her as a twelve-year-old. But if she was alive, she'd be nearly thirty-six by now. She'd have a family, a life.

She'd be Rylie's family. The only living family she had in the world.

Was she still alive?

The resulting search for Maren had wrenched her father into a deep and dark depression. Her took to drink and let their Wyoming Ranch go to pot, so that she'd had absolutely no one except a few kind neighbors on nearby ranches. For college, she'd moved closer to Seattle, to escape the memories of her broken family. But in her heart, she'd promised herself that eventually, she would find out what happened to her mother and her sister.

And so, she did the thing that she thought would keep that promise alive—when she graduated from college, she submitted her application to the FBI.

As she looked around Rylie felt that same feeling of emptiness invading. It was because of that horrible day outside of Yellowstone that she had her career as an agent in the FBI. But other than that, she had absolutely nothing.

That day had taken from her nearly everything that meant something.

She pulled herself up from the sofa and trudged to her bed, to try to get in the next few hours of sleep. But outside, the sky was lightening. The alarm clock on her bedside read 4:31 am.

So much for going back to bed. She'd have to get up for work in another hour, anyway.

Rylie changed into her running clothes so that she could start the day with her usual five-mile run around the streets of downtown Seattle. As she was slipping into her tech shirt, she glanced at her phone, on the dresser. There was a text.

At first, she thought it was Cooper, continuing their conversation from last night. She groaned aloud when she saw Bill Matthews's name on the display. He never messaged her at home.

Great. What does he want from me now? she thought; then her mind went back to yesterday's "pretentious prick" comment.

Her stomach sunk.

This was nothing good.

She picked up the phone reluctantly and opened the message:

Come in ASAP.

She froze. Shit. This *really* was nothing good. In fact, as she went to the bathroom to take a shower, she realized it might mean the end of her career, the only thing she had that meant anything to her at all.

CHAPTER FOUR

Rylie was always in a bad mood when she didn't get in her morning run.

But that Tuesday, as she hurried into the FBI Field Office in downtown Seattle, she felt even worse. She could already feel the noose tightening around her neck.

She was about to go from two standing ovations in one day, to unemployed the next.

He was going to fire her. Wasn't he?

Well, if so, she'd go out with a bang. She'd tell him exactly what she thought of him. She'd already burnt the bridge halfway. She might as well light the whole department on fire, go out in a blaze of glory.

The thing about the field office was that the place was always busy, at all hours of the day. It wasn't a normal, nine-to-five job. So she wasn't surprised to find the place abuzz, even at just after six in the morning.

Lisa Fairlane met her at the door, her face somber. "Oh, Rylie. There you are. Bill told me to send you into his office, the moment you arrived."

"I know," she said, shrugging off her jacket and looking over at Cooper, who was sitting at his desk, flashing her a sympathetic look with those big, baby blue eyes of his.

He gave her a thumbs-up for courage and mouthed, *You'll be all right.*

After their text conversation last night, she'd started to doubt that. And now, as she walked into Bill Matthews's office and found not only his father and Deputy Director Jerry Matthews, as well as Susan Blakely, the head of HR, all sitting along one side of the conference table, she decided she was right to be worried.

"Sit down," Jerry said without niceties as she walked in, closing the door behind her. This definitely seemed like the type of meeting she did not want an audience for.

She did as she was told, sitting in the single chair across from them. She'd never been in one before, but it was pretty clear, by the way they frowned and averted their eyes: This was a disciplinary meeting.

There was a long, drawn-out silence, in which she became more uneasy. If they were going to come down on her, she wanted it done quickly. She wanted to rip off the bandage, so she could know her fate as fast as possible. So she spoke first. "What is this all about?" she prompted.

Jerry Matthews was taller and broader and statelier than the younger Matthews, but age had made most of his face go south, so he had the jowls and sagging features of an old bloodhound. He gazed at her with his sad eyes. "Now, Agent Wolf. I want to start out by letting you know how grateful we are for your service for the past decade. You're an excellent agent with an exemplary track record of getting results, and we're very pleased with that."

She leaned forward. That wasn't what she'd been expecting at all, especially since their expressions and posture told a different story. "But . . .?"

He nodded and laced his fingers in front of him. "Yes. Well, the fact is, we can't cover for you anymore. Your actions, especially of late, have gotten increasingly reckless, and your attitude has been more and more abrasive."

She crossed her arms. "Some people would call it blunt. I call things as I see them. That's an asset."

"Yes, well. It is. But after the altercation you had with Bill, here . . ."

Bill said nothing, simply stifled a smug grin behind his hand and tapped his pen on his blank pad. She stared at him, unable to keep the disgust off her face. "We didn't have an altercation. I simply stated what everyone else in the office thinks, but are too chicken to say aloud."

"Right . . .," he cleared his throat and straightened his tie. "I guess there's no point in asking you to make an apology, because—"

"I don't think one needs to apologize for stating the truth," Rylie said, tapping her toe. *Just fire me already, if that's what you're going to do. Because I'd sooner be homeless than apologize to that blowhard.*

Bill gritted his teeth. "This is bullshit. Dad, just fire her, alr—"

He held up a hand. "Bill, son? Susan? Could you please wait outside? I'd like to speak to Agent Wolf alone."

"But—"

"Bill. Just do it."

Susan got up right up, but Bill did so reluctantly, as if he desperately wanted to stay and witness her being reamed out. Frowning, he went to the door, head down, like a scolded puppy. The door clicked closed behind them.

When they were gone, Jerry finally managed a sad smile. He shook his head. "I know my son is probably not the easiest person to work for. He is trying his best, though."

"I understand that," she said woodenly. *Even though his best is glaringly pathetic and a two-year-old could do better.*

"Then you understand that if it was up to him, you'd be fired."

She nodded. "I thought that went without saying."

He raised an eyebrow. "Is that what you want?"

She shook her head slowly. "You really think that? How could you even ask that? I don't take risks like the one I did for the Edison Blaze case because I want to be fired. And it's not even because I like danger and being reckless. It's because I love the job and want to see justice done."

He nodded, a genuine smile creeping over his face. "That's why we want to keep you. It's not up to him to make the decision as to whether you stay or go. And we want someone who can keep solving these tough cases. You."

She allowed a bit of relief to bloom inside her. "All right. So . . . slap on the wrist? Try not to do it again? Go about your business? Is that it?"

He swallowed. "Unfortunately, no. We can't just let this go. If we do, it'll set a dangerous precedent. And I think this here is simply a powder keg, waiting to blow. Don't you agree?"

She nodded. Her temper and Bill Matthews's insufferable stupidity? Yes, definitely a dangerous combination. "So . . .." she asked, her eyes narrowing.

"So we're taking you off the BAU."

She blinked. "You're taking me off?" She caught her breath. That made no sense. She tried to fit it through her head, but it felt like a round peg in a square hole. "And yet you still want me to keep solving murders? Where are you putting me?"

"We're creating a new unit. You know all about Interstate Route Eighty-six?"

"Well, yes. I should. It goes right through Seattle. Not to mention that I lived about five miles from it growing up, in Montana."

"Right. It starts in Seattle and goes to Eau Claire, Wisconsin, or thereabouts."

She gazed at him. That really didn't make things much clearer. Sure, she liked traveling the country. She'd been in the south, in Quantico, Virginia, for eight months, during Basic Training. But *those* states, those terrible northern midwestern states . . . surely he didn't mean that he was going to send her there? To what was essentially the middle of nowhere? To what she'd successfully *escaped* and had no intention of ever returning to? "What about it?"

"Locals have a bunch of different names for it. But the most common one is the Highway Through Hell."

She nearly laughed. Well, obviously. There was nothing out there, probably, but barren lands. It went through the Badlands, after all, and that was the most accurate descriptor she could give it. Bad. "Why would you . . ."

"There have been twenty-six murders and thirty-three missing persons along that damn stretch of road in the last decade. Every one of them has gone unsolved," he said.

She stared at him. "In the last decade? That many?"

He nodded. "Well, it's hundreds of miles. So it's a long stretch. The FBI has been under pressure for a long time to give some answers as to what's happening; whether it be the work of one killer or many, we don't know. But we have to figure it out. Some of the cases are likely linked, but there's nothing official, so we can't say it's a serial killer. But there's a good chance that there are one—or many-- there. It's a barren stretch of road. Easy for people to get away with crime."

She nodded slowly. It was one of the reasons that her mother's murder and sister's disappearance had never been solved. The campsite hadn't been on 86, but it had been just as desolate. She thought about what she'd overheard the police saying, all those years ago. *We don't have any witnesses. We don't have much to go on. We're sorry.*

"What we really need is someone to go in, as a third party, and look at these cases impartially."

She blinked at those words. It sounded just up her alley, but for one thing. "But . . . Montana?"

He nodded. "And Idaho. And Wyoming. And South Dakota. And Minnesota. And Wisconsin. You'd probably see just as much action as you do now. And I know how you feel about action."

She frowned. "Let me get this straight. You want to pull me from the BAU, kick me down to glorified highway patrol, banish me to a shitty stretch of road in the middle of nowhere? If I didn't know better, sir, it sounds like you're just trying to get rid of me so your son can just continue to foul everything up around here."

His face fell. "Hey. None of that. I understand that you and my son don't see eye to eye. Let's not go into that right now. I'm giving you another chance. It's more than most people would."

She pressed her lips together, thinking. "So these are my only two choices? East Bumblefuck, USA, or don't-let-the-door-hit-you-in-the-ass?"

He nodded. "I'm sorry. My hands are tied. And even that required me calling in favors to the Director out there, putting my own job on the line." He shrugged. "Think of it as a fresh start for you, Wolf. You'll have a new territory, which might be good for you, and of course, we'll cover for you. Say the transfer was your idea. Okay?"

She recoiled as if slapped. "So basically what you're saying is, after ten years of giving you my heart and soul, of bringing to a successful conclusion many cases, my days in this unit are over, and there's nothing I can do."

He nodded, an apologetic look on his face. "I'm sorry."

She snorted and stood up. "Right. You should be sorry for ever putting your prick of a son in this position he's clearly not up for."

"Rylie."

She stopped her fuming and glared at him. Though he was still seated, he somehow managed to stare her down. This was probably what Cooper would call, *Going too far.* She bit her tongue.

"Enough of that. Are you in, or not?"

She scowled. He was playing like he was on her side, but the truth was, he had only one side. His son's. Which meant, he was still against her. That made him even more odious than Bill Fucking Matthews.

"Out. No thanks," she said, thrusting her chin in the air. "I don't like being backed into a corner like this, and I'm sure as hell not going to play any of these games. Goodbye."

And she stomped out of the office, slamming the door behind her. Pride surged through her veins. So what if she was leaving the only job she'd ever loved? It was worth it, just to see the look of horror on Jerry's face.

At least, at that moment, she thought it was. But as she turned around, it hit her. She was unemployed.

Her stomach dropped.

On the way out, she passed Bill, who was smiling smugly.

She couldn't resist. Her temper got the best of her, and she gave him the double-middle-finger salute, before heading to her desk to collect her things.

CHAPTER FIVE

"Did you really have to give him the finger?" Cooper Rich asked, leaning back in his chair, watching her as she piled a few meager personal items into a banker's box—her potted succulent, a photograph from her graduation from Basic Training, her desk calendar.

She was silent, thinking about what else she needed to bring with her.

"Not even just one middle finger." He shook his head. "Two. Geez."

Already feeling the shame creeping in, she said quietly, "You saw that, huh?"

He chuckled humorlessly, "The whole floor saw that."

She looked around. Sure enough, though no one was staring directly at her, they were all tilted toward her, as if waiting to see what train-wreck she'd get herself into, next.

She pulled out a fresh box of paperclips—ha, she'd steal those, and her stapler, just to stick it to them—placed them in the banker's box, and closed the drawer with her hip. "Well, do you blame me?"

He shrugged. "I don't know, I've always wanted to visit Yellowstone, you know. It's gorgeous. So what I'm saying is--out there isn't all that bad."

She stared at him, jaw open. "How did you—" She stopped. His little pay-grade advantage meant he had access to a lot of information she wasn't privy to. "You'd want to go there? Really? Patrol some shitty highway like some kind of traffic cop?"

"Well, all I'm saying is, it's not as bad as you're thinking it is. And personally, I think Hell's Highway needs you."

She glowered at him. "Because I'm the devil?"

He shook his head, stood, and picked up a folder, which he set in front of her. Then he reached into her box and pulled out the stapler, setting it back on the desk. "Because you're a good agent and you get things done."

She took the stapler and started to put it back in the box, but then sighed. If she wanted to stick it to Bill Matthews, stealing a stapler was a pretty lame way to do it. A *better* way would be to make a name for herself, solving the hell out of those cases.

"And it's not like you have family around here. So you're the perfect agent to be relocated."

She glared at him. Way to rub it in. But it was true. She didn't have any family, *anywhere*, actually. The only person she had in her life that she felt like she could count on was Hal, and old rancher in Wyoming. He'd probably love for her to be back in his neighborhood. Even though highway 86 didn't go anywhere near his ranch, she'd be closer to him.

Closer to those memories. To her childhood.

She suppressed a shudder and picked up the folder. "What's this?"

"It's a file that just came across our desk. There was a body found last night near the Montana-Wyoming border. One fifty-fouryear-old woman, Darla McCrea. A mother and grandmother, she and her husband were on a drive to their timeshare in Florida," he said somberly. "She was snatched at a rest stop."

Rylie's heart skipped a beat. It always did, whenever she heard about these things. She opened the folder and stared at the photograph of a kind-looking, motherly woman with blonde curls. She looked like Rose. "And her body was found . . ."

"A few hours later, at a mile marker, farther down the road." He shrugged. "I didn't get a chance to look over all the details, but it's there. The state police called us in to help with the investigation because they think it's related to some other murders around the area."

She glanced over the account of the police officer. The woman had disappeared while her husband was in the restroom. He'd only been gone five minutes, and yet that had been enough. The only trace left of her had been a little blood. And her body had been found, strung up on a mile post near the border. She'd been stabbed countless times.

Rylie's stomach somersaulted as she turned to some of the photographs. They were ghastly, bloody, and even though Rylie didn't have a weak constitution, for some reason, she found them impossible to look at. She didn't realize Cooper was calling her name until he touched her forearm. "Huh?"

"I was just saying that I don't think this is a punishment. They *need* you there."

She looked at him doubtfully. "Nice try."

“I’m serious,” he said with a crooked smile. “If anyone can find out what’s going on and bring some peace to the family of Darla McCrea, it’s you. I truly believe that, Wolf.”

She stared at the folder. All those unsolved cases, including a number of murders. It would be a challenge, if nothing else.

She closed the lid on the banker’s box and offered her hand. “Wish me luck,” she said.

“You’re really leaving?” he asked, disappointment clear on his face.

She hesitated there, unsure, the thought of that woman etched in her head. She probably had a family, and they’d been torn apart. Just like Rylie had been, all those years ago. “Well . . .”

He shook her and said, “Good luck, Wolf. But you’ve never needed that. You’re gonna do great. I don’t doubt it for a second.”

She gave him a scowl and stalked over to Bill Matthews’s office, where he and Jerry were still in conversation, probably talking about hiring her replacement. She pushed open the door. “Fine. I’m in. When do I get started?”

*

When Rylie drove her pick-up close to the Montana border from Idaho, she should’ve been exhausted. She’d been driving for fourteen hours straight, stopping only in parking lots to nap for a few hours here and there. Instead, she found herself energized. She loved being close to the action.

She had a single bag of everything that mattered to her packed in the trunk of her pick-up, and now that she was out of Seattle, she felt very much the same as she had when Dan walked out—like all of those years hadn’t mattered at all. She’d easily sublet her apartment to a college student and put the rest of the stuff in storage, but she didn’t really care if she saw it, ever again. Maybe it was just that she wasn’t nostalgic, or that she was still bitter about Bill Matthews. But part of her wondered if her brain was broken, if she couldn’t care about anything unless it was a horrific crime that needed solving.

Hell, she hadn’t even called Hal to tell him she was heading back east. He’d be thrilled, she knew. But this all felt like a dream, like it wasn’t really happening.

That afternoon, she’d taken the road out of Seattle and driven onto what was known as the North Bend Highway. Or, more ignominiously, Route 86, the Highway Through Hell.

Though she'd tried to nap a few times during the drive, she'd found herself Googling stories about the old Highway. Though it traveled through seven states, it wasn't a main thoroughfare, like many of the interstates. The newer and bigger Route 90, which traveled through some of the same cities, had taken its place. Eighty-six was older, not very well-kept, and only two lanes, in most places. It didn't go directly through any big cities, instead trailing around them, heading through Indian Reservations and remote areas. There were other routes that were more popular and scenic.

And in the last decade, it had only gotten less popular, especially among the locals that lived around it. Some people thought that it was haunted by the spirits of the Natives that had been forced from the land by white settlers. Some people thought devil worshippers found their sacrificial victims there. Some said it was a main route for the slave trade.

Gradually, the long, flat, treeless expanses of yellow gave way to more and more trees, and the signs for the Montana border appeared. Only one state away from Wyoming, her home state.

As Rylie drove, she could understand why it had gotten such ill repute. It was narrow, full of potholes, and had very small shoulders. On each side, large oak trees teemed above, so thick that their boughs almost touched overhead, so Rylie had the feeling she was descending into a long, dark tunnel, despite it being daylight. She could only imagine how creepy it would be in the nighttime.

The more she drove into Montana, the more the condition of the facilities seemed to decline, and the more she felt like she was in another, uninhabited planet. The exits became fewer and fewer, and when she did run across one, all it had was an old, ma-and-pa gas station or restaurant. The places looked a bit questionable, backwoods, with clapboard roofs and boarded windows, like something out of *Deliverance.*

She shuddered, thinking about Maren and Rose and Kiki. The last time she'd seen them, they'd been at a deserted outpost in the middle of nowhere, much like this. Their RV had been one of the only ones parked in that lot, and it was the solitude that had made them all such easy targets.

Rylie glanced in the back seat of her pick-up. She had two banker's boxes there, filled to the top with files about all of the cases from the area. She'd spent the night before she left going through the files, spreading them out on the floor of her apartment, and it was the most horrific thing she'd ever seen. Many young women had been murdered, some children, one man. All of the kidnappings had been women. Some had been shot, some stabbed, some strangled. Some of the bodies had been found on the side of the road, others, buried in shallow graves. She'd tried to connect the dots, but the sheer volume of information had been overwhelming.

Now that she was in the area, though, she hoped she could begin to make some connections.

Unless this was all a dead-end job, Jerry had just been throwing her away, and Cooper was just being nice by saying how much this place needed her?

Probably. But it didn't matter. She was determined to make a difference, no matter what it took. Surging on the gas, she saw the first signs for the Montana border. She'd be at the crime scene soon. She wanted to get through her home state as quickly as possible. She had work to do.

CHAPTER SIX

When she got closer to the Montana-Wyoming border, she shifted in her seat. The next sign said: *ST. XAVIER REST AREA- EASY ON! EASY OFF! OPEN 24HRS! RESTROOMS- VENDING MACHINES! NO GAS! CLEAN!*

That was the last place Darla McCrea had been seen alive. As she passed it, she slowed a little, trying to get a lay of the land. From the road, it was mostly shrouded by trees, but she could see a stout, stone building, set back far from the road, and decaying wooden picnic benches, nearly swallowed up by long grass. There was a police car parked in front, but other than that, the lot was empty.

Her heartbeat sped up. She started watching the mileposts, her breath coming in shallow bursts. *Mile fifty-seven.*

Mile fifty-eight.

Mile fifty-nine.

Mile sixty.

She slowed down slightly as the next mile-post appeared in the distance. As predicted, there was a police car there, as well, and some additional cars, parked half on the narrow shoulder, half on the grass.

Mile sixty-one.

She pulled to the side of the road, behind the police car and a pristine F150 pick-up that looked like it had never done any serious work in its life.

When she stepped out, a tall man with a close-cropped haircut that screamed "former military" walked up to her. He was also wearing cowboy boots, despite his business-casual attire. "Rylie Wolf?"

From his suit and the badge on his belt, she could tell he was one of her own. "Yes?" she asked, confused.

"Hey," he said, extending his hand. "I'm Michael Brisbane. Your new partner."

She shook his hand tentatively. "Ah, there must be some mistake. I don't work with a partner."

He grinned in a goofy, awkward way that made him look no older than a boy of fifteen. "You do now!" Then he quickly sobered and cleared his throat. “Gosh. Uh, this is awkward. I see they didn’t tell you much about this assignment, did they?”

She gritted her teeth. *Damn Bill. Damn Cooper. Damn all of them. They just wanted to get rid of me. What else didn’t they tell me?* Her voice was wooden. “No, they did not.”

“Well, let me fill you in,” he said, walking her toward the milepost. “First, let me introduce you around. This here is Wally Sparks, chief of the Montana Highway Patrol, headquartered over in Smithville.”

A fat, older man in a gray uniform and Stetson lumbered over to her. He had long dark hair and a darker complexion which made her suspect he had Native American blood. “Hey, pretty lady.”

She bristled. The last thing she needed to deal with was more sexism on the job. “Rylie Wolf. FBI.”

His eyes widened. “You’re FBI?” His eyes travelled the length of her body, mentally undressing her. “What’s a pretty little thing like you want to deal with this nasty business for?”

She gnashed her teeth and said in a clipped voice, “Nice to meet you.”

Her “partner” flashed her a sympathetic look and walked her farther down the road. He even walked a bit like a puppet on a string, his long limbs at odd angles. And what was with that constant grin?

“Yeah,” he said, clearly trying to make peace. “So I’ve noticed the people around here are a little backwards.”

Tell me about it, she thought. *Since I grew up here.* Not that she was going to tell Howdy Doody that. He was an FBI agent? He reminded her of Woody from *Toy Story*. Would it be possible to lose him? She was from BAU, so she probably had seniority over him. Maybe she could send him on and “errand” so that he’d stay out of her way.

Rylie drummed her fingers on her thighs, hoping the next stop was the crime scene. Instead, he stopped in front of a black van with open back doors. “And here is Beeker.”

Not the crime scene. Another introduction, and Rylie hated introductions almost as much as she hated Bill Matthews. “Beeker?”

She peered inside the cavernous back of the van to find it full of computer equipment. A kid with bright red hair, standing up on end, and abundant freckles, sat, typing madly. He waved. “Sorry. Hey. Nice to meet you,” he said quickly, turning back to his computer.

“He’s cross-referencing some of the recent crimes in other jurisdictions right now to find any connections. Scott Becker,” Michael explained with a shrug, laughing. "But he looks like the Muppet. So we can't help it. Get it?"

She nodded, conceding that point without joining in the laughter. It felt wrong to laugh, considering what had happened here. Then she noticed that Beeker, too, was wearing an FBI badge. "What is he here for?"

"He's our tech guy."

Great. She had a tech guy, whether she wanted one or not. As much as she probably needed the tech help, did he actually need to be on-site?

And what other baggage were they going to give her? A couple more goofy sidekicks to make the job even more unbearable? She did her best work *alone*. She thought she'd be the sole FBI point of contact on this case. As a woman, she'd always had to work doubly hard to prove herself. Now, likely, all these guys would try to direct the investigation and get in her way. It was always that way—men just made things more difficult. "I'm sorry. Why are *you* here?"

He laughed in a good-natured way. She had to admit, despite his Woody look, he was also somewhat attractive, like a young Robert Redford. He was probably used to getting people to follow his lead, which made her dislike him all the more. "I'm actually here from the Missoula Field Office. I've been an agent fifteen years. I'm their top cold-case investigator. So they selected me specially for this role. Coffee?"

Fifteen years? He was probably a GS-14, too. But *she* was supposed to be their lead investigator on this. She frowned, wondering what step he was on, so distracted by all this new information that she didn't realize she'd already accepted the mug of coffee he thrust in her hand. She took a sip of the bitter liquid, swallowing hard.

He sat on the back bumper of the van. "So, what's your story, Agent?"

She glared at him. "I didn't realize this was story time."

A smile spread across his face. "I feel like we're going to get awfully close on this detail. We might as well know a little something about each other."

"Close? No thanks."

"All right. Then . . . fine. Tell me something. Right now, all I know is that your name is Rylie Wolf."

She let out a sigh, trying to determine what he needed to know. That was *all* she'd tell him. "Fine. I'm from Seattle. I've been an agent for ten years, working for the BAU," she said absently, scanning the area. "I'm sorry, Agent . . ."

"Brisbane."

"Agent Brisbane. Right. Would you mind showing me the scene so that I can get up to speed on this?"

He sprang up. "Oh. Of course. Let's go this way." He motioned her around the car and paused. "I should warn you. The details of this case are a little—"

"Agent. Seattle is no playground."

He nodded. "Uh, yeah."

He led her alongside the line of cars, on the grassy part instead of the shoulder, since the speed limit around here was seventy, and a walk on the other side was too close for comfort. When he reached the mile marker, he said, "This is where the body was found. One Darla McCrea, fifty-four, from Spokane, Washington. Last seen at the St. Xavier Rest Area, which you probably passed a few miles back."

The body had been removed, but there was crime scene tape around the area. Other than that, there wasn't much to see. "Can I take a look at those photographs?"

"Uh, yeah. The police just handed me this." He held up a folder. "Just warning you. I kind of . . . some of even the more experienced officers around here had quite a reaction to it."

"I'm fine. I saw them already."

She reached for it, but at the last second, he snatched it back. She glared at him as he said, "All business, aren't you, Agent Wolf?"

"What else is there?" she said shortly, swiping at the folder again.

This time, he let her take it. "All right, all right. Don't get anything twisted. I was just . . ."

Seeing if I had a sense of humor? Well, I don't. Not when there's a murder to be solved.

She opened it to find a report, and scanned it. "And how much time elapsed between when the woman was kidnapped and when she was found?"

"Not much time at all. In fact, the police received 9-1-1 calls about it even as they were responding to the call from the husband."

She frowned. "How is that poss—"

"Motorists thought it was a dummy. A scarecrow or a mannequin, propped up on the side of the road. They called it in. It was because the body wasn't just dumped. It was set up, on the mile marker, tied to it, presented like a sacrifice. She was brought here, tied up, and strangled."

He motioned to the folder. She flipped to a picture of a woman, strung up against the mile post, like a human sacrifice. She noted the thick ligature, tied around the victim's neck. Her head lolled to the side, frosted blonde curls covering most of her face.

Rylie fought the urge to wince. "There were others similar to that, weren't there, along this road? I remember seeing them in the files."

He nodded. "That's right. Not exactly like that, though. There was a prostitute in Wyoming that was found by a milepost, but she'd had her throat slit, and it looks like that was done by one of her johns. They're all a little different. It's as if the killer knows we'll be coming up with a profile and changes things a tiny degree, every time, so we never can definitively tie any of these together. There are a lot of cases to go through, though."

"Sounds like an inside job. So you have been coming up with a profile?"

He shook his head. "That's the first step. The police didn't do much of anything because the killings have been spread out along the six-hundred-mile route. Different police jurisdictions. It's only recently they started to put two-and-two together. That's when they called us in. I myself just got here last night."

That made Rylie feel a bit better. She hated walking into a party late. She studied the photograph, noting the woman's clothing was intact. "Ever any sexual assault?"

"Sometimes. Sometimes not. In this one, no. No DNA. The killer's always clean."

Rylie raised an eyebrow. "That's bizarre. That sounds to me like a group of people. You know, united in a purpose, but each individual crime perpetrated by someone in the group."

Brisbane nodded. "Yeah. Could be. At this point, anything's possible."

"And the murder seems very odd, because look at the way her hands are out," Rylie said, pointing to the way they'd been pulled back. A strange feeling of déjà vu crept over her. "It looks religious in nature. Like someone was trying to emulate a crucifixion."

Brisbane shrugged. "Could be."

"It reminds me of something, but I can't say what."

Rylie knelt by the place where the victim's body was found, noting the disturbed dirt and footprints on the shoulder. By now, a hundred rescue workers and police officers had been here, disturbing the crime scene. She referenced the photo, where the earth had been marked with long dark, haphazard ruts. "There were signs of a struggle. So he killed her right there, on the side of the road?"

Brisbane nodded. "Yeah. You can tell she was dragged out there, by these two marks, which were heel marks," he said, pointing. "But then she must've started fighting back. So she died right here, on the side of the road. I bet a bunch of cars passed by and had no idea. It's dark, the speed limit's seventy. They probably didn't even know what was going on."

Rylie suppressed a shudder. "Tells us the guy's not afraid of getting caught. Anyone could've driven by and seen him."

And that meant they were dealing with a serious madman. Rylie flipped to a picture of the woman—she looked very much like Rose, the all-American, pie-baking mom, who went around in an apron and had no enemies. Of all the killers she'd dealt with, they had a reason for their actions. They'd felt wronged by the victim, wanted to keep their victim quiet, or something like that. Edison Blaze had a racket, selling kids for cash. But never before had she dealt with a killer who murdered people for no reason other than the sheer pleasure of it, the challenge.

She stared at the photograph of Darla McCrea, standing beside a tall, gray-haired man in a t-shirt and cargo shorts. They were standing in front of a harbor, between two palm trees . . . in Florida, it looked like. He looked to be a bit older than Darla, though still fit and attractive.

"This is . . ."

"That's Calvin McCrea. The husband."

"Where is he? I'd like to talk to him."

Michael gave her a strange look. "Me too."

Oh, right. He was her *partner*. She needed one of those like she needed another hole in the head. In Seattle, they'd started her out with a partner, but she'd quickly shaken that one. The man was older—he couldn't keep up. Afterwards, she'd had a string of forgettable partners that proved to be no better. Most only lasted a couple months before requesting a change.

Not her fault. She was sure of it. A person didn't join the FBI unless they were prepared to deal with pressure. She put pressure on her partners, and if they couldn't deal with it, it wasn't her problem. She only had one rule when it came to working with her—*Do it the right way, or else.* And as far as she was concerned, the right way was always hers.

Michael Brisbane, with his bad haircut and his happy-go-lucky attitude, wouldn't last a week. He was too soft. He'd cracked cold cases? Doubtful. The best thing about him was his charming smile. Missoula had probably been *itching* to get rid of his useless ass.

"And you're in luck. Because I just asked Wally about him a minute before you got here. Calvin McCrea was at the state police office until early this morning and they're keeping him at Shady Bend, next exit. You can follow me over, if you'd like." He dug his hands into the pockets of his slacks and smiled. "And something tells me with you, it's the sooner, the better. Am I right?"

She nodded. "That's right, Agent, and don't you forget it. Let's go."

Though she had to admit, she'd already forgotten his name.

CHAPTER SEVEN

Riley quickly realized that the Shady Bend Resort was not a resort at all. It was a ten-room, one-floor motel that looked like something out of *Psycho,* and right off the highway, the kind of place people rented by the hour, or in the dark of night, when they were so tired from their travels they didn't care where they rested their heads, since they'd be motoring on at daybreak.

Rylie parked her pick-up next to her partner's black sedan. He'd already gotten out and was standing near the chain-link fence by a sad-looking pool, half-filled with a murky brown miasma of leaves and filth. A sad, half-inflated elephant pool ring bobbed mirthlessly in its depths.

"Want a swim?" the agent teased, picking up a loose stone beneath his loafers and tossing it, rippling the once-calm surface.

She scanned the rooms. Each one had a mustard-yellow door, and a single picture window in front, but some of them had been boarded up. "Which one is McCrea?"

"Ah, right," he said, motioning with his chin to the last one, number ten. "That's the one."

She took the lead, marching over to it and knocking on the door.

A moment later, a weak voice called, "Who is it?"

"Mr. McCrea?" she called through the door. "It's Agent Wolf, from the FBI. And . . ."

She glanced back at the agent, who gave her an odd look before responding, "Agent Brisbane."

Right. That was his name. "We're investigating your wife's death, and we were hoping to speak with you. Do you mind if we come in and ask you a few questions?"

A moment later, the door opened. The man she'd seen from the picture appeared, wearing the same t-shirt and cargo shorts, his eyes much more bloodshot, and his smile gone. His hair was sticking up, and when he opened the door, a side of the bed was rumpled, suggesting he'd tried to get some sleep.

A musty, moldy smell struck her, the second she stepped in. The place was dank and unwelcoming. She hesitated. "Would you like to step out and get some fresh air?"

Calvin McCrea nodded wordlessly and followed her outside. There was an old picnic bench near the road. She sat there, and Brisbane straddled the bench next to her.

"First," Brisbane said, taking the lead before she could. "I'm sorry for your loss."

He nodded absently.

"Yes, we're both very sorry about your wife," Rylie said quickly, trying to get the first question in before he could. "Can you lead us through exactly what happened, in your own words?"

He put his elbows on the pitted surface of the rotted wood table and buried his face in his hands, rubbing his eyes. "What good will it do? Darla's gone, and I couldn't save her. She didn't want me to stop, but I had to. This is all my fault. And I've already told the police—"

"I get it, man," Brisbane said, reaching a hand out to him. "It's hard. I know this is the last thing you want to do. But it's helpful to us. It is. The first time you told it, you were in so much shock, you might've left things out. This time, if we take it from the top, we'll get a clearer picture and it'll just get us closer to catching this creep. All right?"

McCrea's fingers spread, and his eyes landed on the agent. He nodded. "All right. Like I said, we weren't supposed to stop. Darla was always afraid of something like this happening. She planned everything, to a tee, right down to our bathroom breaks. But I had to pee. I couldn't wait another second. So I pulled up to that rest stop, that damn, lonely rest stop, the St. Xavier one, and I told her I'd just be in and out. I meant to be."

Rylie nodded. "And were you?"

He shrugged. "For the most part. The lights were flickering, so that was kind of weird. They were motion sensor, and I suppose the sensor wasn't working right. And then I thought there was someone in one of the stalls, watching me. Turned out to be a janitor. So after that, I went in, did my business, got a Coke, and came back. And she was gone."

"And—" Brisbane started, but Rylie spoke over him.

"How much time passed from the time you left the car, until the time you returned?"

"Maybe four, five minutes?"

"You didn't hear anything going on in the parking lot when you were in there?" Rylie asked, on a roll, now. "Maybe another car, pulling up? Voices?"

He shook his head. "Nothing. Nothing at all. There was water dripping in one of the sinks, and it was pretty loud. I didn't hear anything else."

"Did you see anyone at all, besides this janitor?"

"No."

"And the janitor . . . did you speak to him?"

"No. Not at all."

Brisbane nudged her and showed her his notepad. Scrawled on it were the words: *Ernesto Rodriguez, janitor,* and some contact information. They'd have to speak with him later. "Did you see where the janitor went?"

"He stayed in the restroom the whole time I was there, and when I left, he was still in there." He sniffed.

"Did your wife get out of the car to stretch her legs or anything, use the restroom, too?" Brisbane put in.

He shook his head. "She was afraid to. When I got out, I flipped the locks so she'd be safe. It was really dark and she didn't want to be there. So I made sure she was safe. That's why I can't understand how this happened. She was locked in. And she wouldn't open the door for just anyone . . ."

Rylie paused, thinking. She'd locked herself in. And she was afraid. So either she'd thought it was her husband, returning, and had opened the door, or she'd gotten out for some other reason.

And Darla McCrea was a planner. A control freak. She liked things just so. People like that were often very hard to live with.

Theories swarmed her head, but it was a wild, improbably idea that planted itself in her brain. She pushed it away, but it kept returning with force, along with the Arthur Conan Doyle quote: *Once you eliminate the impossible, whatever remains, no matter how improbable, must be the truth.*

Darla had locked the doors. She wouldn't open them for just anyone. She was controlling. He'd gone against her carefully laid plans. They might have argued, and . . .

Brisbane had taken over the interrogation, thoroughly asking question after question, but she was no longer listening. He went on, asking the typical questions about what happened next and whether he remembered seeing anything out of the ordinary at the stop, but Rylie's mind had gone off in another direction entirely.

"What was your itinerary like?" she blurted, while Brisbane was in the middle of asking another question.

Brisbane stopped and both men looked at her. McCrea said, "What?"

"You said your wife was a planner. Where were you planning to stop?"

He paused. "We had a reservation at a Holiday Inn, I think. I don't know. The police took all that in as evidence."

She studied him carefully. Likely story. Perhaps he'd put together this little trip for the sole purpose of murdering her. People could be so cruel, so calculating. Or maybe he hadn't planned it at all. Maybe it had just happened. But so many times, when investigators looked for a "crazed madman who kills for the sheer pleasure of it," they should've been looking closer to home, for someone who had a very good reason to commit the act. Spouses were *always* a good possibility.

"I saw in the report that the truck had no sign of forced entry. So I'm just hung up on how you say she was so afraid that she locked herself in, but somehow, she'd opened the locks herself to let a crazed murderer in."

McCrea stared at her, confused. "I—I don't know. It was dark? Maybe she thought it was me, coming—"

"Or maybe she knew her attacker?" Rylie said.

"That's ridiculous. We don't know anyone here. We're—" He stopped as realization dawned. "What are you saying? That I did it?"

When she didn't say anything, horror crept into his face.

His mouth, wide as an O, hung like that for a full ten seconds. "My God . . . are you saying that I'm a suspect?"

Brisbane shook his head. "That's just one possible explanation of a thousand," he said diplomatically, side-eying Rylie. "Of course, we're not saying you're a suspect. But we have to explore all possible avenues. We want to catch your wife's murderer as much as you want us to. And to do so, we mustn't leave any stone unturned."

McCrea nodded, but gave Rylie a glare. "I understand. I appreciate you."

Rylie sucked in a breath. *Well, aren't you Mr. Sunshine, partner?* She already got the feeling that her new partner went through life, caring more about being liked than about getting results. And that wasn't the way she operated. So what if she ruffled feathers, if she got her man in the end? "Fine. Obviously, the case is new and we're obviously looking into a number of possibilities. Can you think of an instance in which she might be forced to open the door for someone?"

When McCrea turned to her, his frown deepened. "Well, yes. If the assailant was armed and threatened to hurt me, she might. She was always so protective of me, always so . . .." He buried his face in his hands and began to sob. "I can't believe she's gone."

Her face fell. If he was acting, this was Oscar-worthy. Though spouses were often the perpetrator in murders such as these, she got the definite feeling she was barking up the wrong tree. Brisbane gave her a hard glance, confirming it, and stood up. "Thank you for your time, Mr. McCrea. We won't bother you anymore."

"I just have a few more questions," Rylie said, trying to be more positive.

"No, we don't," Brisbane said under his breath, heading for the parking lot.

"I do," she said, looking over her notes. "It won't take long. I have here that you left Spokane, Washington, a couple days ago, on the route. Can you give me a little accounting of what your trip was like, up until you arrived at St. Xavier?"

Brisbane heaved a sigh and sat back down on the picnic bench, leaning forward, away from McCrea, with his elbows on his knees.

The husband nodded. "We always like to take our time when we head to Florida. To enjoy the sights. So we go different ways, in order to see things. She wanted to see a fountain, and then we stopped in Missoula to do a little antiquing, and then she wanted us to go to the Buddhas, because she said that would be nice." He laughed to himself. "She had all these ideas. I just went along for the ride. I might've been at the wheel, but really, she was the one driving."

"And so before you got to St. Xavier, when was your last stop?"

His rueful smile faded and his brow wrinkled in concentration. "Somewhere in Montana." He shook his head as if he couldn't remember, and she thought he'd say so. But suddenly, it must've come to him, because he held up a finger. "I remember. It was a Dairy Freeze Service Station. Somewhere on the road before Missoula. I remember it because that's where I saw that nice truck. Mean trucker, though."

"There was a mean trucker?" she asked.

Now, Brisbane was interested, because he turned to face him. "What about the trucker?"

Calvin McCrea nodded and looked down at his hands, which shook a bit. They were the hands of someone who did a lot of manual labor, gnarled and worn. He said, "It was probably my fault. Darla said never to talk to strangers. People are just too unstable these days. But he had a nice truck with a custom paint-job on it. A desert scene. I'm an automotive guy. I liked it. So I tried to tell him. He was out there, looking under the hood, so I went over and said that he had a pretty sweet set-up."

"And?" Brisbane said, now keenly interested.

"Well, he damn near jumped down my throat. Told me to back off. I told him I didn't mean any harm and just wanted to pay him a compliment, but he was having none of that. He reached into the pocket of his flannel shirt and my life flashed before my eyes. I thought he was going for a gun."

That was a promising lead. "What did this person look like?"

"He had long, greasy hair, kind of light. I think he had a scar on his chin. Blue baseball cap with what looked like a blood on it. Flannel. Jeans. His truck said he was based in Montana. That's all I remember."

Rylie looked over to see Brisbane scribbling all this down. "Back up. Blood? You mean, his hat was covered in blood?"

"No. It looked like a logo. Like a droplet. Of blood. On the front. You know?"

Rylie shook her head, but Brisbane nodded. "Okay, I think we've got what we need."

This time Rylie lifted up from the bench, thanked the man, and handed him her card. "We'll keep in touch. And please, if you think of anything else, don't hesitate to call us."

They walked back to their cars. Rylie was just about to comment on the blood on the hat when McCrea said, "That was harsh."

"Huh?"

"Your way. It was a little . . . harsh."

"It gets results."

"I know, I know. But you catch more flies with honey, you know?"

She stopped. "That might be your way. But my way is what got us the lead. What are you saying?"

He shrugged. "I'm saying that it doesn't hurt to be nice and sympathetic to people."

She sighed. He was probably right, but she wasn't about to admit it. Not when they were hot on the trail of a killer. Besides, her way got cases solved. She wasn't about to change it now, especially where a sadistic murderer might exist. They sure as hell didn't deserve sympathy.

"I'm doing my job." She pointed to the car. "Would you like to follow me to this Dairy Freeze Service Station, or should I follow you, Agent?"

"Why don't I just drive and then I'll drop you off back here once we finish?"

She nodded. As he went to his car, he shook his head and muttered under his breath, "And it's Brisbane."

*

On the way West to the service center, Rylie started to regret letting her new partner drive. It wasn't just the terrible country music he put on or the fact that the inside of his car looked and smelled like a showroom, indicating that he was even more of a perfect goody two-shoes than she'd suspected. Mostly, it was that the entire time, he wouldn't shut up.

"So, you're from Seattle? You ever been to this part of the country?"

She shook her head.

"You like it here? I bet it must be a far cry from rainy Seattle? It rains a lot there, huh?"

She shrugged.

"I bet it must be pretty different. Gotta tell you, this ain't much different from where I grew up outside of North Dakota. Well, I moved to the east coast and started in Virginia after basic training in Quantico. You were in the BAU, right? I thought I read that?"

She nodded, not really listening anymore.

"Yeah, well. I moved back west a few years ago. Been back in Missoula ever since. This is a good change of pace, you know? Always good to open your eyes, see what else is out there, you know?"

"What about that janitor?" she suddenly said.

He paused, sidetracked. "Oh. You mean Ernesto? Nothing. They questioned him. He doesn't even speak English well, so he wasn't much help."

She frowned.

"You ever been up to Yellowstone?"

She glared at him.

"Okay, I'll take that as a no." He drummed a hand on his thigh. "I didn't get to travel much as a kid. I kind of want to make up for lost time. This country's great. I want to see it all. You know?"

She nodded, glad that though he'd asked about a thousand questions, most of them really only required a nod. She squinted into the distance, where the road went on, flat and treeless, disappearing into the distance. "Where is this place, do you think?"

"I know where it is. Southeast of the reservation. We should be there in about fifteen minutes," he said, lowering the volume on some sad country crooner, making her cringe, because she knew another long line of questions was coming next. "So, what? You live in Seattle all your life? You like it out there? You have to deal with a lot of murders out there, I bet, huh? If the weather's bad, I bet so. I've noticed people are more likely to commit crimes when they're depressed, you know? Though that doesn't make much sense for Florida. Florida has the nicest weather of any place, and the most crazies. You notice that?"

She was glad he kept asking questions, not pausing to allow her to answer. He was one of those people who could probably carry on a conversation with a wall. Sure enough, they arrived at the service station, without her ever having to reveal a single thing about herself.

As they pulled up near the intersection with Interstate 40, Rylie remembered passing this place. It was the biggest service station for miles, with a giant MOBIL gas sign visible far in the distance, and a lot with dozens upon dozens of trucks, lined up outside. One half was devoted to filling up, the other half was a diner, with a small convenience store in between. "This place sure is hoppin', huh?" Brisbane said as he stepped out. "I'm dying for something to eat. Haven't had anything since breakfast. You want to get something to—"

"I'm not hungry," she said, walking at a purposeful clip across the lot as she checked her phone. It was only three in the afternoon, and he was boo-hooing about missing lunch? They clearly went too easy on agents in North Dakota.

When she reached the line of trucks, shielding her eyes from the sun with her hand, she scanned the area for the truck in question. She didn't see anything matching Calvin McCrea's description of the flashy, custom-painted truck. These were ordinary. As she stood there, a truck driver honked at her.

At first, she thought she was in his way, so she started to move off, but then she caught him waving at her with a toothless, leering grin. She rolled her eyes and reversed direction, hurrying into the diner.

"So we are getting food?" Brisbane asked, catching up with her. "Hell yeah."

The diner was busy, every booth full. It didn't matter. She wasn't planning on eating, no matter what her partner wanted. She strode up to the center island, which was surrounded by a counter, and slid onto the only available barstool, between two truckers who were shoveling in their meals.

A waitress with a bright-orange dye-job and spidery, long fake eyelashes came up to her. "What can I get you, honey?"

She reached into her pocket for her credentials. "Nothing, but I was wondering if I could ask you—"

"Yeah, I'll take a burger and fries, and a vanilla shake," the order came over her shoulder. She looked over at him to find her partner shrugging.

"I'm hungry," he explained, muscling in between her and the trucker. The trucker, annoyed, pushed his plate away, laid a twenty down, and walked away. He slipped onto the stool and drummed his hands on the table as the waitress headed off.

Rylie had been wanting to ask her a question, but now, she was busy with other customers. She glared at Brisbane. "Seriously?"

He shrugged innocently. "Well, I—"

"When she comes up, could you please let me do the talking?" Rylie asked, as nicely as possible. Some of the truckers around the area looked mean as hell. She wanted to get in and out of this place, as soon as possible. If her partner would let her.

He nodded and plucked some napkins from the dispenser. "Sure. Whatever you say."

CHAPTER EIGHT

If there was anything that could make life miserable, it was a bad partner.

Brisbane knew this, better than anyone. He'd had his share of difficult colleagues, and he wanted to make sure this relationship didn't go south on the very first day. He wanted to give her the benefit of the doubt, after their rocky start where she'd looked at him like a glob of gum on the bottom of her shoe.

So he pressed his lips closed and tried to let Rylie Wolf, the pretty little spitfire who obviously hated him, take the lead.

Why did she hate him? Had he done something to her? He usually got everyone to like him. That was his superpower. So was there something wrong with her . . . or with him?

She was clearly comfortable in the driver's seat. He got the feeling she'd never had a partner before, with the way she talked over him and practically ignored him, much of the time.

Too bad. She was pretty. More than pretty. Gorgeous. She had this long, thick dark hair and light eyes he could get lost in. She dressed in a no-nonsense way, with no frills, and yet she still managed to look distinctly feminine. She even smelled good. If this weren't business, if he'd seen her in a bar, he'd have made it a point to walk across the floor and talk to her.

But he'd never had much luck when it came to love, and this just proved it.

Rylie gave him a look that said she wished he didn't exist and spun on the stool. Then she said, "You stay here. I'm going to ask some of the truckers if they remember seeing that guy."

She slid off and walked away without waiting for a reply. A moment later, the waitress came back with his shake. Brisbane checked her nameplate—Marnie.

"Thanks, Marnie," he said, and flipped her his ID as he took a sip. "You've probably been working here a long time, huh?"

She nodded. "Honey, I've been here since the dawn of time. At least, it feels like it." She winked.

"You probably see all kinds of truckers in here?"

She laughed. "Do I! My first and third husbands were truckers. Sweetie, I've seen every kind of trucker known to man. I got them coming out my ears."

"So you wouldn't remember one in particular, then, probably?" he asked.

The waitress batted those long eyelashes, charmed. "Oh, try me. Every trucker has his flair."

"You remember a guy with an Oklahoma City Barons baseball cap on? Blue, with a copper-colored—"

"You mean Mac," she said. "We all know Mac."

He perked up. "Yeah? He's a regular?"

"Oh, yeah. Comes by this way with his rig at least once a week."

The big, bearded guy two stools over spun. "Mac? What's he done now?"

Marnie shrugged. "I don't know, Hal, but the Feds are after him. So it's got to be pretty big business."

Hal, who was probably twice Brisbane's girth, and Brisbane had never figured himself for a lightweight, looked him over and guffawed. "I figured the Feds would come on out on the Highway Thru Hell one of these days. What with all that stuff going on. But I never thought Mac would be a part of it."

A couple of other truckers, seated around the U-shaped counter, were now listening. "So what's Mac wanted for now?" a tall, skinny guy said.

"He's just wanted for questioning for a case. That's all. Anyone seen him lately?"

Marnie nodded. "Saw him day before yesterday. He was in a bad mood. Didn't even give me a tip."

Tall-and-thin laughed. "When's Mac not in a bad mood? And he's stingy as all hell, too. No tip? Marnie, that's a travesty."

Hal nodded. "Yeah, he's known for having something crawled up his ass and died. Permanently. If he did anything, I want nothing to do with it."

"Yeah, me neither," tall-and-thin said, dropping a few dollars on the counter and pushing away.

The cook passed a plate over the pass-through and rang a bell. Marnie delivered the burger. As he was dousing his fries in ketchup, Rylie appeared behind him. She looked pissed, and as Brisbane turned, he could see why. A couple of truckers were catcalling her, blowing her kisses.

He smirked. “You have fans. I think they’re in love.”

She curled her fingers into a fist. “If they keep at it, they’re also going to have my fist in their face.”

She said it with such seriousness, he didn’t doubt it. After her play with McCrea, openly suspecting him of murdering his wife, he wasn’t sure he could trust her to keep a lid on it. He pointed to the seat. “Sit down. Sure you don’t want lunch? My treat.”

Rylie shook her head sullenly. “I want answers.”

He stared at her, hardly able to believe her. Hell, this girl was all-business, no soft spot whatsoever. Didn’t she ever stop talking about her job? It intrigued him, the way she’d artfully ignored his questions. It made him want to try harder, to get to know what was under her skin. “And you didn’t get any?”

“No. This whole trip was completely unhelpful. No one seems to know the truck I’m talking about. What about you? Did you learn anything?”

He motioned around him. “Yeah. These people know the guy. His name’s Mac . . . Mac . . .?” He glanced at Marnie. “Have a last name to go with that?”

Marnie shrugged. “Ain’t much use for last-names around here.”

Rylie looked at him, confused. “How did you . . . they knew his truck?”

“No. They knew his hat. With the OKC Barons logo on it.”

“You mean . . . the blood?”

He nodded. “Oil, actually.” To her astonished expression, he explained, “I’m a bit of a hockey fan. I figured that’s what McCrea was talking about when he described the hat.”

“Oh.” He didn’t expect a “good job” from Rylie, and he didn’t get one. She simply nodded and looked at the waitress. “When was the last time—”

“Day before yesterday. We covered that,” he said, a little smug, since she’d clearly been prodding him along because she thought he was the one wasting their time. “None of these guys seem interested in saying much about it.”

Marnie shrugged. “Can you blame us? This here’s the Highway Thru Hell. Anyone who stops around here don’t stay long. They get through this place as fast as possible.”

Brisbane chewed on his burger. “You’ve been here a long time.”

"That's because I'm not afraid of the ghosts and curses and bad stuff they say lingers around here."

Rylie leaned against the counter. "Curses?"

Marnie laughed. "Oh. Yes. The land here's part of the Trail of Tears. The highway follows one of the original routes some of the Natives took when they were expelled from their homelands. There's a legend that goes that a Cherokee chief cursed the route so that they wouldn't be followed and forced to move again. It said that anyone who stopped there would be doomed to death."

Brisbane studied her, feeling an icy finger curl down his spine. Rylie rolled her eyes. "Everyone is doomed to death, eventually. It's actually one of the few things that's one-hundred-percent certain." She pulled out her pad and read her notes. "Do you remember seeing Mac leave? Do you have a time on that? Direction he was headed in?"

"It was after the dinner rush. And he went east."

East. That meant he'd been following the McCreas. "Do you recall seeing him getting into an altercation with a tall, balding man of about sixty, in the parking lot?"

She tapped her chin. "As a matter of fact, I do! Mac just doing typical things Mac does, making trouble. He was carrying on so loud, yelling and screaming. I remember feeling sorry for the poor woman that guy was with. She looked mortified, and I couldn't blame her. I wondered what that was all about, so I asked her."

"Oh. They came into the diner?"

"Yep. Sat right on over there in that corner booth," she said, motioning to the far end of the restaurant. "The husband had chipped beef and the wife had chicken and dumplings, light gravy."

Brisbane nodded. "Wow. Your memory is astonishing. Is there anything else you can remember about them?"

"Tipped well." She shrugged. "That's all I care about."

Brisbane looked around and realized that most of the truckers that had claimed to knowing Mac had suddenly taken off. They really wanted nothing to do with the man. "Do you happen to know when Mac might be back?"

She laughed. "I don't keep track of their schedules. But he'll probably be back around sometime in the next five days, on his return from wherever he went."

Rylie slumped over the stool. "Five days? Great," she muttered.

"I wish we had some way of getting in touch with him," Brisbane explained to the waitress.

Marnie pressed her lips together, thinking. "Oh. I do know what trucking company he works for. Arrow, out of Oklahoma City. Does that help?"

Brisbane polished off his burger and nodded, grabbing his phone. "Now I think you're onto something."

He started to unroll his napkin so he could wipe his hands and not grease up the display on his phone, when he looked over and saw his partner. She already had her phone up to her ear. "Hi, this is Rylie Wolf of the FBI. I need to ask you some questions. Do you have a Mac that works there, that has a route through Montana and was in the area two days ago?"

She listened for a moment, then grabbed a napkin and a pen from her purse and started to scribble something down. "Yes. That's right. Where is he right now? Okay." A pause. "No, that's all right. Do you have a cell phone number or some way we can get in touch?" She scribbled something else down. "Thank you."

She hung up and held the napkin triumphantly. "Clive McDougal." She slipped off the stool. "Let's go. I'll call him from the road."

"Do you know where he is?"

"Somewhere near Missoula. They won't give me an exact," she called over her shoulder, pushing open the door. As she did, a trucker coming in gave her a wolf whistle. She threw them the finger.

Brisbane quickly threw a twenty down. "Thanks, Marnie."

"No problem, sweetie," she called after him as he jogged to keep up with Rylie.

When he caught her, she was holding the phone to her ear and pacing. Then she looked at the phone, jabbed a number, and did it again. "Dammit. He's not answering!"

He motioned to his F150. "Get in. I'll call Beeker and see if he can do anything."

While they were driving, Brisbane pressed a few buttons on his dashboard and the display there lit up as the call was connected to Beeker. The kid was barely twenty-two, just out of the FBI Academy, and was the typical computer geek who didn't have much in the way of social graces. But he was brilliant, and sorely needed on the force. "Beek. It's Michael."

"Hey, Bris. Where you at?"

"I'm back on my way heading toward Missoula. Can you help me out, though? Can you get into a trucking system's navigation grid?"

Laughter. "Dude. I can hack into anything."

“That’s not legal, Beek.”

“Oh, stop being such a goody-goody, *Bris,”* Rylie muttered, rolling her eyes. “It’s a matter of life and death. Beeker, can you get into the Arrow trucking system and find out where a Clive McDougal’s truck is? We think it’s somewhere near Missoula.”

“Sure can. Hold on a sec,” he said.

Brisbane looked over to find his partner sitting there with a sour look on her face. No doubt, she wanted to be the one to move this case along. What a piece of work.

“Bris? I’ve got it. He’s heading east from Missoula now on Eighty-six. Looks like he’s stopping at the Sugar Grove exit.”

“Great. Thanks.”

Brisbane disconnected the call and pressed on the gas, ignoring the grumpy looks from his partner. They had to get to Sugar Grove as soon as possible.

CHAPTER NINE

Rylie tapped her fingernails on the armrest and glared at Brisbane as they headed down Route 86.

"Do you think you could possibly go any slower?" she finally asked, after shifting in her seat and groaning and trying to make her displeasure known less vocally.

He glanced at her. "What do you mean?"

"I mean that you drive like an eighty-year-old. Didn't you have defensive driving in the Academy?"

He nodded. "Of course. We all did." He pointed to the speed limit sign. "It says seventy. I'm going seventy."

She sighed, "That's just a guideline. You can go much faster than that."

"Guideline?" His eyes narrowed, in the same way Bill Matthews's had when she'd asserted the FBI rulebook was just a guideline, too. "Who the hell taught you how to drive? Limit. *Lim. It.* Meaning, your speed does not go over it."

"Okay, maybe, but who's going to pull us over? We're FBI. And we have business to get to."

"And as an FBI agent, more than just upholding the law, is *adhering* to it." He seemed disappointed in her. "Don't you believe that?"

"Of course I do. But not when we're trying to catch a killer. When we're trying to catch a killer, we can go at least ten miles over the limit."

He seemed to consider this. Then he patted his steering wheel lovingly. "I just got this truck two months ago."

"So? She's a fine truck. Stretch her legs. Let's see what she can do!"

He nodded and pressed down on the gas. Now, instead of going seventy, they were going seventy-two.

She groaned.

"Do you want me to drive?" she asked.

He dipped his sunglasses and gave her a look that said it was the last thing he wanted her to do.

"I'll have you know I was first in my defensive driving class," she said, even though it was a lie. The truth was, she'd never crashed a car, in all eight months of Academy. That was something.

He motioned up ahead with his chin. "We're almost at the exit."

Sure enough, the sign for Sugar Grove came up a moment later. When they pulled off the highway, they found themselves at a small outpost that had nothing more than a gas station and a Subway, semi-attached to it. There were a few trucks parked behind the station.

They pulled into the parking lot and climbed out of the pick-up, looking for the purple truck with the desert scene on the side. As they were looking around the lot, a purple truck with a desert scene on the side sailed down the street past them, heading for the on-ramp to the highway.

"There!" Rylie shouted, but Brisbane was already running. She reached the front of the truck. "Give me your keys!"

He didn't have time to argue. He threw her the keys. She caught them, got in the cab, and revved the engine, then pealed out, onto the road, kicking up gravel.

The tires squealed as she made a hard right and sailed up the on-ramp, after the truck.

"Whoa," Brisbane said, white-knuckling the handle on the door. "Take it easy."

"I *am* taking it easy," she said with a grin, loving the way the new truck handled. It was much nicer than hers, and she'd always had a thing for fast cars and big pick-ups, just like her father. But she didn't really have time to play with it. They had a trucker to catch.

She punched the gas, leaning on it, hands gripping the steering wheel, and still, she wasn't going fast enough. Luckily, it was a semi she was chasing, and semis couldn't hide and could only go so fast. She came up to its rear bumper fairly quickly, flashing her headlights to it to get it to pull over.

The driver seemed to step on his own gas and surge forward.

Letting out a frustrated groan, Rylie quickly swerved into the left lane, but the truck moved over too, riding down the center of the highway. She rode half in the left lane, half on the median, trying to come up beside the cab.

"What are you doing?" Michael asked, horrified.

"What does it look like? Trying to get him to pull over. When we get even with him, flash him your badge, okay?"

She easily pulled up until she was even with the cab and he did as she told him. Still the truck continued. She honked her horn, then laid on it, trying to get him to move off.

"This isn't working."

"Yeah, it's not. Let's rethink this," he said, still gripping tight to the seat. "We should call in reinforcements."

That was the last thing she wanted to do. That was like admitting she couldn't handle something on her own. "No! Please, we've got this."

Driving side-by-side on the highway, she waved her hands frantically. Brisbane had taken to staring in horror at what was ahead of them, his feet up on the dashboard. "Watch—"

A car was meandering along in the slow lane, ahead of them. Without warning, the truck veered off to the right, driving on the shoulder, to pass it. The car slammed on its brakes as the F150 sailed past it on the left and the semi passed on the right, kicking up a cloud of dirt.

"We are going to die," Brisbane said matter-of-factly, squeezing his eyes closed.

She scoffed and upshifted, speeding up as the truck made its way around the slower car and pulled back onto the road. "Oh, my God, Agent. This is nothing. What do you do on a daily basis in North Dakota? Go on picnics?"

"We don't drive like nutcases," he said through gritted teeth.

"He's not going to stop," she muttered under her breath, gnawing on the inside of her cheek. "I have to try a new tack."

"A new . . .," He reached for his phone. "I got it. How about if I call the police. Maybe they can put a roadblock up ahead."

"No time," Rylie said, checking in her rearview mirror, then looking up ahead. It was clear. They could keep going like this, until the pick-up ran out of gas, if she didn't think of something. Which would be . . .

She glanced at the gauge and frowned. Really? It was almost on E. The "low gas" light was on.

"Agent. Seriously? Why didn't you fill your tank?"

"I'm sorry. I didn't know I'd be chasing down an eighteen-wheeler today," he retorted sourly, still stiffly watching the road ahead through half-closed eyes.

"And here I thought you were a Boy Scout. I thought you would be prepared for this kind of thing!" she muttered, still staying neck and neck with the truck. "Okay. Ready? PIT maneuver."

"What?" he glanced at her in shock. "With a semi going eighty? Are you insane?"

Her heart was pounding, her face hot. She glanced at the rear-view mirror. "What else can we—"

"STOP!"

She saw the brake lights up ahead just in time. The traffic jam took up both lanes. Slamming on her brake, the pick-up truck fishtailed, tires screeching, coming to a stop mere feet behind the last car in the jam.

They watched in horror as, unable to stop in time, the truck sailed off onto the shoulder, knocking an exit sign over and flattening a mile marker, then careening across a grassy field, burrowing deeper and deeper into the dirt before it came to a shuddering stop, hood partly buried in upturned earth.

"I feel like I'm going to be sick," Brisbane mumbled, powering down his window and gasping for air.

As the dust settled, Rylie squinted to see the truck, watching for any movement.

Suddenly, the door sprang open, and a wiry man in a t-shirt and jeans appeared and started to climb down from the cab. He was wearing the blue baseball cap.

"There he is! He's on the move!" she shouted, throwing open the door and jumping out onto the highway. The traffic was hopelessly stopped, because people had gotten out of their cars and were congregating at the guardrail, watching. She was vaguely aware of Brisbane opening up the passenger side door and following her, but by then, she'd raced over to the edge of the road. Sure enough, Mac was running across the field, dodging in and out of the scrubby bushes, trying to escape.

Fumbling for her gun, she pulled it from the holster and took aim.

"FBI! Freeze!" she shouted, but it did no good.

She jumped into action, scrambling down the steep embankment to the field. She launched herself over a bush and sprinted after him, quickly making up ground. Mac wasn't the most athletic of people, because she quickly bridged the distance. When she was right on his tail, she shouted at him again to stop.

He didn't. He looked over his shoulders, and in his face, she saw the wild eyes of someone who would do anything to escape.

"Stop! Now! This is the FBI!"

Just as she was about to lunge after him, though, he turned to bolt away and misjudged his step, because he went flying over a small rock in his path. He fell on his hands and knees, and she went stumbling after him. They wound up in a tangle of limbs, and when she looked for her gun, it was gone.

A second later, her partner was there. "Got this," he said, as if it were nothing. He easily overpowered the wiry man, grabbing him from the back of his t-shirt as he took the cuffs from his belt.

She found her gun in the weeds and holstered it as Brisbane grabbed him by the arm, wrenching him around, letting her fall to the ground with a thud.

She stared up at him as he got the driver into position to cuff. "Clive McDougal? You're under arrest."

At the guardrail, about fifty yards off, a small audience began to applaud and holler. "Way to go!" someone called. "Get 'em!" People were capturing the whole thing on their phones, and she could just imagine this getting back to Seattle—her partner making the arrest while she landed in the dirt.

"What the hell?" she shouted at her partner as he snapped the cuffs on one wrist, and then the other.

He glanced at her. "I think the proper phrase is, Thank you."

"Thank you!" She stared at him, speechless. "For what? Getting in the way?"

He snorted. "I don't know. You looked like you were in trouble."

Out of breath, the suspect's shoulders slumped. "I didn't do nothing. I don't know where she came from."

Rylie muscled her way over to the man and pulled him to standing. "Where *who* came from? The woman you killed?"

Without warning, he hung his head and began to sob like a baby.

She stared at him. Hardened serial killer, he was clearly not. He looked like he was in need of serious mental help. Brisbane said, "I'll call the police so they can take care of this jerk," and wrenched him toward the highway.

"Wait. I want to question him, first," she said as he led him off. She matched their pace. "Why did you do that to that woman? How many other people have you killed?"

"I didn't kill no one," he said between sobs. "I didn't. I swear I didn't."

So he's going to play it tough like that, even after bawling like a baby in front of us. Perfect.

Brisbane led Mac toward the truck to wait for the authorities. Luckily, they didn't have to wait long, because as they reached the side of the road, police sirens screamed in the distance. The traffic jam was probably the result of an accident, up ahead, and they'd already been called to that.

As they climbed the embankment, Rylie hung back near the truck, stranded in the middle of the field. Sure enough, the desert scene on the side of the truck cab was distinctive. The door was open, so she wrapped her hand around the handle on the side of the cab and pulled herself up.

The cab smelled like cigarettes and old coffee, but it was a luxury interior. The seats looked like new leather, and there was very little in the way of trash—just an empty coffee cup in the console. For someone who spent his life in this cab, he did keep it very neat.

She crawled in farther and turned her head to look between the two front seats.

And that's when she saw it. A tanned, slim leg, slightly bruised.

She pushed aside a blanket and saw a girl of no more than eighteen, with messy hair and bloodshot eyes, gagged with what looked like a dirty rag. Her limbs had been bound. She gazed back at Rylie with pleading eyes that seemed to say only one thing.

Help.

CHAPTER TEN

Rylie sat in the back of the ambulance with the girl as she was checked out. Aside from a few bumps and bruises, she appeared to be in good shape. At first, she was trembling, clearly traumatized. One of the police officers brought her a bottle of water, and after she took a few sips, she seemed to break out of the trance she'd been in.

She looked nothing like Maren, with her dark, stringy hair and tanned limbs. And yet, Rylie couldn't help seeing her sister. Maybe Maren had suffered a similar fate, bound and gagged and hauled off . . . but they would never know that. At least this girl's story would have closure.

"Do you think you can talk?" she asked gently.

The girl nodded. "Are you an FBI agent, really?"

Rylie nodded. "What is your name?"

"Ava. Ava Kowalski," she said softly, gnawing on her chapped lower lip.

"Age?"

"Sixteen."

"Where are you from?"

"Sedalia, Montana, ma'am," she said politely, twisting the water bottle in her hand so that the plastic crunched loudly.

"You're a runaway?"

She nodded and dropped her chin to her chest. "My boyfriend and me were heading to California in his car. But we got in a fight. He got cold feet and decided to go back. I told him to drop me off in Kansas City, and I started hitching my way across."

"When did you meet Mac? Mr. McDougal?"

"At a truck stop in Salina, Kansas, ma'am." She swallowed. "He offered me a ride and promised to take me all the way to Denver. But then he started driving the wrong way. Said he knew a shortcut if we went North. I believed him at first, even though he was being creepy. Putting his hand on my knee and stuff like that. But when we reached the Montana border, I knew something was wrong. I told him to pull over and let me out, and so he did. But then he grabbed me. He tied me up and put me in the back of his truck. I was so scared."

"I know, I'm sure you were," Rylie said, giving her a reassuring smile. "But you're safe now. Your mom and dad are probably worried about you."

Her brow wrinkled. "My mom. I ain't seen my dad since I was two."

"All right. The ambulance is going to take you to the hospital, just so a doctor can check you out. You think you should call your mom and have her meet you there?" Rylie took out her cell phone and handed it to the girl, who nodded.

"Yeah," she said sheepishly. "I guess I should. Thank you. Thank you for finding me. I don't know what would've happened if you didn't."

"I hate to think," Rylie said, giving her a bony shoulder a gentle squeeze.

She jumped from the back of the ambulance and saw Brisbane, standing in front of the open back door of the police car, speaking with another officer and the suspect. When Brisbane saw her, he motioned her over. As she approached, he stepped aside and whispered in her ear, "This guy's looney tunes. I don't think this is the only girl he's kidnapped."

If they were looking for a serial offender along the highway, this sounded promising. A thought of Maren flashed in her head as she stepped between the officer and Brisbane and found Mac slumped in the back of the squad car, cuffed wrists, on his knees shaking uncontrollably. "You've kidnapped other girls?"

He nodded. "I like girls. They like me."

She crouched in front of him. "Tell us about these girls."

He smiled, a sadistic smile that chilled her. "I think God puts them in front of me, to tempt me. So I have to pick them up. God knows the kind I like. Dark hair, dark eyes, limbs that go on for days. When I see one, I can't resist picking them up."

That didn't sound much like Darla McCrea. "And then what do you do with them?" Brisbane asked.

"I take them to a hotel. We spend the night together. We have fun. Then I let them go." He shrugged as if he'd done nothing wrong. "I don't kill 'em, if that's what you're looking for. I ain't no murderer."

"Kidnapping an underage girl is a crime, sir," the police officer said.

Mac shook his head, as if he believed the law was wrong and it shouldn't be. "They ain't hurt. They enjoyed it."

Brisbane scoffed. "You actually believe that girl you kidnapped enjoyed being tied and bound in the back of your truck? You're sick, man."

"A lot of us truckers do. I ain't the only one. It gets lonely on the road."

"Yeah? Who else do you know who takes girls?"

He shrugged. "You think I'm going to rat them out? You're wrong. I don't know nothin'."

But Rylie wasn't concentrating on that. Yes, Mac was a despicable criminal. Yes, he deserved to be behind bars. But they were investigating the murder of Darla McCrea. And though Mac might've been doing wrong, he was starting to sound less and less like their suspect.

"Do you know Darla McCrea?" she asked.

He gazed at her with disgust in his eyes. "Who?"

"Fifty-four? Curly reddish hair? She was at the Dairy Freeze Truck Stop the last time you stopped there, outside of Missoula."

More disgust filled his eyes. "Why would I . . . is she dead?" He smiled. "And you think I did it?"

They didn't answer.

He laughed. "Sorry. You're barking up the wrong tree, agents. That ain't me." He lifted his bound wrists to scratch the side of his grizzled face. "Oh, I remember that old gal. Ugly fat cow. She and her stupid, nosy husband. Am I right?"

Rylie frowned.

"Now I remember her. Only because that husband of hers was trying to get a look in my cab. I told him to back the hell off. Didn't want him getting in the way of my fun with pretty Ava. But you're definitely on the wrong track there, girlie. I drove on to Cheyenne that night. Stayed at the Whippoorwill Motel on 40. I didn't go anywhere near Route 86."

Rylie turned away and stalked back to the truck. It all made sense. He was a criminal. Just not *their* criminal. She gazed along the Highway Thru Hell and sighed. There had been dozens of crimes committed along its length, so she couldn't have expected them all to belong to the same person. There were bad people everywhere, out there.

It chilled her, though, to think of all the people on Earth with evil in their hearts. Sometimes she wondered if those people outnumbered the good, and if that was the case, what chance did this world have?

CHAPTER ELEVEN

Every masterpiece took time and planning. All the great artists knew that.

Mile fifty-seven.

Mile fifty-eight.

Driving down Highway 86, coming across the St. Xavier rest stop, he smiled.

Oh, he'd had his fun, there.

He'd seen her, in Montana, at the Dairy Freeze. He'd stayed at the gas pump, waiting and watching for her. She had pale, pale skin, the perfect contrast to the red of her hair, to the red of the blood he'd soon spill. It would be explosive. Never-before-seen. She'd be more beautiful in death than she ever had been in life.

The old woman had been stupid. As scared as she'd been when he pulled up behind her, he'd easily won her over.

He could do that. Despite all the bullshit his father had spewed about him being a worthless good-for-nothing, he'd gone to school, made something of himself. He was good-looking, smart. He'd spent years, cultivating his charm, just for this.

All he'd had to do was tap on her glass, ask her if she knew how far Rapid City was. She'd tried to roll down the window, but with the car off, she couldn't. She'd cracked open the door, and the rest was history. He'd powered his way in, grabbed her, made her his.

Mile fifty-nine.

Mile sixty.

The man's heart pounded like a drum. *Mile sixty-one.*

Mile sixty-one.

And there it was. Half-hidden by a commotion of police cars and news reporters, it had been a bit of a masterpiece. The way he'd spread her out there, it was pure poetry. If he could've taken a photograph of it, to save and tote around in his wallet, he would've. She'd looked better than in life, hanging there, bleeding.

It felt like he was getting better and better at it, every time.

Soon, he would be perfect.

Soon, he would create the spectacle that no one on earth would miss, that would make them all stand up and take notice of him. And then he'd reveal himself, take ownership of it, and they would stand in awe of him. His name would be plastered everywhere.

Mile seventy-six

Mile seventy-seven

Mile seventy-eight

A flutter of excitement passed through him as he imagined the sight. His breathing became shallower and he wrapped his hands around the steering wheel as he pulled off at the exit for a place called Fort Winston. This exit, right before the town proper, was isolated, with a small donut shop on one side of the road, a gas station on the other.

He pulled into the gas station and parked, got a terrible coffee from the convenience store, and sat there, watching the shop. From this place, it was almost too far to see much of the donut shop. The gas station attendant had been facing away from it. Across the street, the parking area was off to the side, away from the entrance of the shop, and there was no drive-thru. There was only one person in the place, manning the counter, a pimply face kid who was playing with his phone, looking bored.

It would be perfect.

Pulling out of his parking spot, he smiled, his skin prickling with excitement. He couldn't wait for the fun to begin. This was such a desolate, ugly stretch of road, with nothing beautiful for miles and miles. A shame, really. He'd grown up here, and had always thought so.

It could use some brightening up.

CHAPTER TWELVE

Three hours after their stop in the Dairy Freeze diner, at six in the evening, Rylie actually *did* begin to get a little hungry.

However, now that they'd solved one crime and had a little break, she figured she should probably stop for a bite before she passed out from lack of food. She felt antsy because she'd missed her morning run, and hadn't eaten at all since she'd stopped for gas that morning at the Idaho-Montana border and gotten a candy bar.

"You know of any place good to eat around here?" she asked him as he drove. She noticed that he kept looking down at the steering wheel, as if he could detect she'd done something terrible to the truck while she'd been behind the wheel.

He looked up. "You really want to eat?"

"Yeah. But you're probably not hungry, since you—"

"No. One thing about me is, I'm always hungry. You like steak?"

She nodded. "But I'd rather just get something quick, since—"

He veered to pull off at the next exit. "You will not have a better steak than at Howdy's. Trust me."

"Howdy's?" Well, that suited him just perfectly.

He nodded.

The day had been long and tiring, and she didn't have it in her to argue. She kept thinking of poor Ava, hoping she would soon be reunited with her mother and that she never got it in her head to go hitchhiking again. Ava had been lucky; she was one of the very few who'd been found. It was far too easy to disappear from this world, without a trace, never to be seen again.

When she blinked again, she realized they were in the very busy parking lot of a large building, done up like a log cabin. The insides blazed with light, and she could already smell the mouthwatering scent of cooked meat and potatoes. Brisbane was already stepping out. He snapped his fingers at her. "You thinking about that girl, huh?"

She nodded.

"Yeah. That was something. I've never seen anything like it."

She wished she could say the same. She'd seen plenty of harrowing things, but it was always the young girl kidnappings that hit her the hardest.

She pulled off her seatbelt, stepped out, and joined him on the front porch of the restaurant. Luckily, it was after the dinner rush, so they were seated right away. The place was the kind of establishment with farming implements and photographs on the walls, where people threw peanut shells on the floor and got their hands sticky with barbecue sauce. A lot of the patrons were wearing cowboy hats.

"Is everything all right?" he asked her as they sat.

"Sure. Why wouldn't it be?"

He chuckled and set his napkin on his lap. "I don't know. I mean, that might be who you always are. But you seem a little distant."

"I'm just used to working alone."

"Yeah, all right, I got it. But I'm not so bad. You might even find I can be of a little help, if you need it." He winked. "I mean, that's what I meant to do, when I got that guy. Didn't mean to step on your toes or anything."

She frowned. The waitress came by. She ordered an iced tea and opened the menu, hoping to keep the conversation at a minimum. "It's fine."

"So, what made you want to become an FBI agent?" he asked, leaning forward.

She sighed. She really didn't have it in her to carry on with this. "You know what? I really don't have the energy for small talk. It's been a long day. And we might be partners, but we really don't have to know everything about each other, do we?"

He stared at her for a moment. He didn't look hurt, or angry, or anything, which almost made her dislike him more. He simply nodded, "Fair enough."

Her iced tea came. She took a long sip of it, feeling more and more guilty. Cooper would tell her that she was being rude. And she was. No wonder they'd banished her from the Seattle field office and hadn't called to check in with her once. She didn't exactly give anyone warm fuzzies.

"Now you look like you're thinking on something else," Brisbane said.

She looked up to find him studying her intently. "What are you, a psychologist?"

"I thought you would appreciate it, being BAU. You analyze behavior, don't you?"

"Of potential criminals. *Not* my partners, Agent."

His eyebrows shot up. "Oh, so you're finally admitting I'm your partner? Even if you still don't know my name, that's progress."

She frowned. "I do. It's Michael Brisbane. And I never said I was against having a partner. I just said I was used to working alone. And I've never really had one." *That stayed around very long.*

"You didn't have to say it. Your actions spoke it pretty well. And to tell you the truth, I'm not sure I've done anything to deserve you shutting me out. If I'd done something out of line, or I screwed up, yeah. But I haven't. In the end, Agent Wolf, we both have the same job. I want to find out who did this as much as you do. And I'm not going to stand for someone getting in the way of me doing my job, even if it is my partner."

She stared at him, stricken. She was about to snap something mean about how he'd stolen her thunder at the last apprehension, but, she realized, he was right. It was his job, too. She'd been stepping on his toes just as much as he'd been stepping on hers. They were supposed to be working *together*.

As much as it sucked, she had to admit, it would probably make things easier if she just let him help.

She sighed. She had a tendency to do things like this—have tunnel vision about a case and forget all about how other people perceived her. "I'm sorry if I've shut you out."

He shrugged. "It's all right. I just think that we could work better together if we, you know, learned to trust each other a little bit."

She stared at him, doubtful. Probably the reason why she never had a partner is because she'd never believed any other person could truly have her back. Since Maren's disappearance, she'd always been suspicious.

And it wasn't just that. In her head, she still believed that this was a mere speed bump, and it was only a matter of time since she was back in her office in Seattle. She still thought of this as temporary, even though Bill Matthews hadn't so much as said Boo to her since she left. He hadn't done a single thing to check in and see how the investigation was coming along, and he usually kept a close eye on all of his agents. Yes, the prick was probably celebrating her departure. But she hadn't even heard anything from Cooper, either. It was like she was out of sight, out of mind. She couldn't exactly see them turning around and welcoming her back with open arms once all this was over, even if she went and solved every single murder along this godforsaken highway.

She hated to admit it, but it was almost like they didn't care. They didn't care about the murders. They didn't care what happened to her. And they didn't care if she came back. It was almost like this was . . . permanent.

With that, her spirits sunk even more, and she buried her nose in the menu. *Steak. A big one. And enough mashed potatoes to drown myself in.*

The waitress came, and she ordered her steak and potatoes, and then handed her menu over. Then she leaned in, and whispered to him, "I always thought FBI agents were cool."

So what if it wasn't the truth? At least it was an answer.

His eyes went up in astonishment. He laughed. "Yeah?"

She shrugged. "You wanted to know why I became an agent."

"Yeah. Well, cool. Me too. When I was a kid, I watched that movie *In the Line of Fire* with Clint Eastwood? I thought nothing could be cooler than Dirty Harry. But then I saw that movie, and I was *sold*."

She smiled. "I've actually never seen that movie."

"What? As an FBI agent? Well, it's a good flick. You need to. Harry Connick Jr as a serial killer? Doesn't get much better than that," he said, drumming his hands on the table. His smile fell, and his voice turned serious. "Look. I know how you're feeling. We thought we were close to finding some answers, and now, we're left without any leads."

"We need more to go on," she said. "What about the janitor?"

"Dead end. Like I said, the police interviewed him. Not only does he not speak very good English, but he had his earbuds in and says he didn't hear or see anything."

"There's got to be someone who saw something. I know 86's not the most traveled highway in the state, but the killer took care in stringing the body up there on the mile-marker. I can't believe he did it without anyone noticing it. Did they get the names of the people who called it in?"

"No. And no one else has come forward," Brisbane said with a sigh, leaning back and straightening his tie. "So I think the only thing we can do is be vigilant and wait."

"For what? The killer to strike again?"

He shrugged.

She winced. Waiting was a terrible idea. The worst. "I don't like that. There must be something we can do. Did Beeker find any past cases that might be similar?"

He shook his head. "He's still looking. Not much in the database. So far, each one's just different enough that there's no way of comparing them. But he'll keep at it."

"I'm going to look through the files tonight."

"I can help. I think whoever the killer is, he's smart. He knows how to cover his tracks and keep us guessing."

"So we just have to sit tight and wait for someone else to be murdered." She looked around, her appetite gone, just as the waitress arrived with two heaping plates of steak and potatoes. The smell made her stomach roil, thinking of the way that poor woman had been carved up, like some kind of sacrifice.

She wished she could be outside, on the highway, searching. At least there, she might have a chance of catching this killer in the act.

*

By the time they finished dinner, it was after nine. In her mind, Rylie had this grandiose idea of patrolling the highway, looking for the killer in the dead of night, but Brisbane was right. There was too much ground to cover for that to do any good, and it was so dark that any efforts would be difficult. Her best bet was to sit down somewhere quiet and look through those old case files.

The closest hotel was across the street, a neat little Best Western with horseshoes on every door. As they walked into the office, she looked up at the elevated highway 86, watching the taillights trail into the distance. Any one of those people could be killed, or a killer. There was just no way of knowing.

Yawning, she rang the service bell and laid her elbows on the counter. When the clerk, a young woman with a nose ring, came, Rylie said, "One room, please."

The young woman's eyes shifted to Brisbane. "For the two of you?"

Rylie blinked, suddenly awake and so surprised by the question, she couldn't answer. "Oh, uh—"

"No. Two rooms, please," Brisbane spoke up, taking out his wallet. "If they can be close together, that would be best. And on the first floor."

She glanced at him. "Do you need someone to comfort you if you get nightmares, Agent?"

He chuckled. "No. But those case files look heavy. And if I'm going to share the load with you, I think we should probably be near one another."

"You don't need to. You're tired," she said as the clerk handed over their keys. "You should just get some sleep. I'll let you know in the morning if I find anything."

"Oh, no. I insist." He smirked at her. "This is my investigation, too, Wolf."

Right. She'd resigned herself to remembering that, but still, she'd much rather have gone over it all, alone. Even so, they wound up having rooms on the first floor, just steps from their vehicles, so it wasn't too difficult to lug the files in. He helped her pull all four of them into her room, and the boxes were stacked on the empty double bed.

"You want me to start with this box?" he said, lifting up the lid on the first one. "I can take it to my room."

"I'd prefer all the files stay here," she said, shrugging off her jacket and stretching her arms over her head.

"Why, Wolf. Are you trying to get me to spend the night with you?" He smirked.

"No," she said pointedly, rolling up her sleeves. If he weren't here, she'd have changed into her comfy sweats and put her hair in a messy bun by now. "But it was my field office that went through the trouble of compiling the files, and so I'd rather keep them all together. So sit over there."

She pointed to a round table in the corner, far away from her. He grabbed the first file and opened it. "Fine."

She sat on the edge of the bed, donned her reading glasses, and opened another file, pulling out a case file for a murder that had happened in Montana. A woman had been beheaded by an unknown assailant, the body left on the side of the highway. She scanned it carefully, looking for any definitive ties to the Darla McCrea murder. Other than the woman being about the same age, nothing jumped out at her.

As she moved onto the next file, she looked up at Brisbane, who was scanning his own file, a look of mild disgust on his face.

And who could blame him? One file after another detailed some horrible crime, committed on the area highway. Homicides, missing persons, possible suicides, kidnappings, sexual assaults . . . each one more horrific than the next. Even if she hadn't been struck by personal tragedy, it was hard not to be jaded by this business. But despite all this, her partner was rather happy-go-lucky. She had to admit, it intrigued her.

Stop, she told herself, forcing her concentration on the files. *You don't need to be thinking about him when you have a murder to solve.*

After that, she kept her head down and crawled into a rabbit hole. By the time Rylie had gotten another file in, her stomach swam with nausea. People could be so sick. So depraved.

She was roused from those disturbing thoughts by an obnoxious, duck-like honking sound that nearly made her jump straight out of the bed.

Then she saw Brisbane, head tilted back, mouth open, fast asleep.

She rolled her eyes, smiling. It was nice to see that he wasn't perfect. But this wasn't exactly the best bedtime story. She'd likely have nightmares, tonight, like always. She always had dreams of that day in the RV, of hiding, as the rain fell, listening to the faraway gunshots. . .

He let out another long snore, enough to wake the dead, and it roused her from her bleak thoughts.

"Hey. Brisbane," she said, looking for something to throw at him to wake him up. When she couldn't find anything, she decided to let him sleep, despite how grating the sound was.

She opened another folder to the case of a fifteen-year-old girl named Chrissy, who'd disappeared about a year ago. She had long dark hair and a similar look to Ava. The last time she'd been seen had been at the Dairy Freeze Diner, where she was asking truckers for a ride. "Hmm," she said, paging through the file. "I wonder if Mac had anything to do with this girl's disappearance?"

In response, Brisbane let out another long snore.

She shuddered as she looked at a photograph of the girl, and thought about how her sister would stand in the sun, outside the bullet RV, in her little belly-baring shirt, dancing to her favorite Spice Girls songs while she and Kiki clapped along.

Maren.

Each of these files contained one nightmare after another, and had resulted in so many lives, destroyed forever. No, Rylie would not be getting any sleep tonight, not when all the while, the murderer could be out there, taking his next victim.

CHAPTER THIRTEEN

Tonya Birch yawned as the next road sign came into view:

I-86 12

Good. Next stop, her home state of Wyoming.

Montana was so damn boring. There was nothing to see, nothing to do, nothing but bare, dark expanses on either side of her. Even the music on the radio had gone from some cool, rockin' nineties pop songs to stuff that even Lawrence Welk wouldn't deign to play.

Her foot had gone numb and lazy on the gas pedal, and her speed had gradually decreased. Now she was only going fifty-five. She pressed on the gas and got herself back up to seventy. Twelve miles to I-86, then hang a right on I-25 toward Casper, and then another sixty miles beyond that, her hometown of Douglas.

Hallelujah.

She yawned, anticipating that blissful moment when she'd be able to collapse into her nice, warm bed. The thought made her even more tired.

Whoa, wake up, she thought, slapping her cheeks a little.

She went to reach for her commuter cup, and frowned. It was empty.

She'd filled it hours ago, when she'd left the hospital in Billings. But she'd been drinking it steadily, and had finished it before she crossed the Montana state line. Usually, it was enough to keep her awake so that she could make the long drive back home after her Billings shift.

But this day had been pretty crazy. It had been non-stop running, dealing with all kinds of crazy things.

Tonya looked up at the white disc in the sky. *Ah. Full moon. Now it makes sense. All the weirdos come out on the full moon.*

She had been a travel nurse for three years, ever since she'd graduated from the University of Wyoming with her RN degree, but she couldn't remember being quite this tired.

She laughed to herself. *You're just turning into an old lady. At twenty-four! Get a grip!*

Mentally trying to do the math to determine how long it would be before she got to her home, she frowned. Her brain was fried. Grabbing her phone from the center console, she punched in a call to Hilary.

She answered on the third ring. "Hey, roomie!" Tonya said brightly. "Are you still up?"

"Barely. You coming home tomorrow?"

"Tonight! I'm only a little ways out. Just about to cross over the Montana-Wyoming border. So, probably another few hours. But I'm totally dragging. Keep me up?"

A laugh. "How?"

"I don't know. Amuse me!"

"Why don't you stop and get a coffee?"

She drummed her fingers on the steering column. "I would, but I think I've already had too much. I'm jittery."

"Okay. Oh! I have something I wanted to tell you. Guess who stopped by."

"Who?"

"Robbie."

"No!" Tonya gasped, a little thrill traveling up her spine. Robbie was the med student she'd met in college. They found out that he lived only about twenty miles from her place. He was shy, and their schedules kept them apart, but the last time they'd gone out, Tonya had a definite feeling like he wanted to take their casual dating relationship to the next level. "What did he want?"

"He didn't tell me. He said he was sorry he missed you, and he'd call you tomorrow."

"Ooh," she said with excitement. "I wonder what that's all about."

"You'll find out soon enough."

"I guess. I really can't--" she started to say *wait*, but the word got caught in a giant yawn.

"Wow, girl. If even Robbie news won't keep you up, you're in definite trouble."

She meant to blink, but her eyes closed for a bit too long. She had to pry them open. "Seriously."

"Get a coffee. You'll never find out what Robbie has to say if you're crashed in a ditch somewhere."

"True," she said as she spotted the exit for Fort Winston. Two miles away. A second later, another sign appeared: *FOOD: The Happy Donut Café.*

That has my name written all over it, she thought, as she eased off the gas.

"All right. I'm at an exit. I'm going to stop and get coffee. And then I'll be home in another couple of hours. You don't have to wait up."

In response, Hilary yawned. "It's two a.m. Believe me. I won't!"

That made Tonya yawn even more as she ended the call and threw her phone in the cup holder. As the exit came closer and she veered off the ramp, she frowned. The Happy Donut had sounded so, well, happy. Like a place where nothing bad could exist. But now, as she pulled to the stop sign at the end of the ramp, a chill went down her spine.

The place was a dinky, dirty, dark hole in the wall.

Well, that's Wyoming for you.

The convenience store near the gas station across the street was even worse.

All right. I'll just pull in, get my coffee real quick, and get out, she thought, navigating to the parking lot. Oddly, there were no spots right near the entrance—she had to park in a lot behind the building, rather far away from the front door, which was only steps away from the road. As she pulled past the door, she peered inside. It looked empty.

The lot, too, was empty. So it wasn't exactly a hotspot. Didn't matter. Even bad coffee would be welcome at this point.

She pulled her Honda into the closest spot to the road and stepped out. As she did, she looked around. The lot was bordered on two sides by dark, empty fields that stretched out into the distance. Tonya shivered, feeling as though someone was watching her.

Shaking that feeling off as paranoia, she rushed to the door and practically threw herself inside.

She practically jumped out of her skin when a voice called, "What can I get you?"

It was a teenage boy with an acne-scarred face. He looked less-than-happy to be helping her. She noticed the phone in his hand; she'd probably disturbed his viewing of whatever was on there. Somehow, even this pimply little kid seemed sinister.

"Coffee," she said quickly. "As big as you have."

He poured a rather small cup for her. No matter. At that moment, all she wanted to do was get out. Pushing it over the counter, he said, "Anything else?"

She shook her head, already digging through her purse for the coins. Not finding anything smaller, she handed him a twenty, then looked over her shoulder, wishing she could see her car. He took far too long, counting out the change.

Normally, she put cream and sugar in her coffee, but a bit of instinct struck her at that moment, and told her not to wait. She thanked the boy, pocketed her change, and took her coffee. Stepping outside, she looked around. It was so dark. The lights in the gas station across the street seemed to glow in an otherworldly way. But in the darkness of every corner, something moved. *Was* someone watching her?

She brought the cup to her lips and took a sip, forgetting that it was too hot. It scalded her lips.

"Hell," she said aloud, hurrying to her car.

The path to it seemed to stretch out in front of her like a bad dream, where every step forward only took her farther away. The air had a distinct chill to it that made her every pore prickle.

Or was someone there? As she picked up the pace, somewhere, an owl hooted. When she reached the edge of the building, she half-expected some masked figure to jump out at her.

Of course, no one did.

She let out a breath of relief as she pulled open the door and slid inside. Pulling the door closed behind her, she concentrated on her coffee. She pulled off the lid and inhaled its lovely scent.

Come to mama, she thought to herself. *You are just what I need to get home safe and sound.*

Suddenly, a hand shot out from behind her, wrapping itself around her and sending the coffee flying against the driver's side window and her arms. She let out a squeal, more of surprise than of pain, because the pain really didn't concern her. At least, not as much as the hands, wrapped around her throat, quickly stealing all the air from her lungs.

CHAPTER FOURTEEN

Michael Brisbane was in the middle of a dream. He knew it was a dream, because it was too perfect—when would he ever get the time out of his job to walk along a tropical beach with a strange, beautiful woman in a bikini? And yet he chose to indulge the dream, the warm sun, the sand, the woman's sexy laughter ringing in his ears as he pulled her close.

Suddenly, though, the sky clouded over and a tidal wave appeared in the distance.

His first instinct was to run. He turned to the beautiful woman, and her features morphed into the face of someone familiar. Her lips twisted around the word: "Michael!"

"Michael!"

He blinked and found himself under a bright light, in a strange, stuffy motel room. Looking around, he realized he'd fallen asleep on a case file, and there was a long line of drool dripping from his chin to the page. Wiping it off, he looked around for the tidal wave.

Instead, he saw his new partner, Rylie, frantically waving a file in front of him. "Michael! Wake up!"

Shit. Where the hell was he? Where was the beautiful woman? Well, his new partner was a looker, but she didn't look like the type to wear a bikini. And when had he rented this crap-hole hotel room?

He looked everywhere but at his partner, trying to find the woman in the bikini, but slowly the realization dawned that it was a dream. There was no tidal wave. No beach. No beautiful woman.

He was so depressed by the news that he almost closed his eyes and tried to go back. But then he remembered why he was here. He'd been sent up to investigate this case, and all the other cases, along the desolate Route 86. This was what he lived for.

And his partner had just made a discovery.

"What?" he said, rubbing his eyes to get them to focus. "Did you find something?"

"Yes!" she said, spreading the open file folder in front of him. "Look at this. The case of Nancy Sharpe last year, in Boles . . . do you know where Boles is?"

He nodded. "Yeah. I think it's east of the I-25 exit. What is it?"

"Well, look. She was a prostitute, and she didn't have any family begging that the case got solved, so the local cops dealt with it the best they could and it just kind of went away. The report itself isn't very thorough, but one part of it did stand out to me," she said, pointing to the police report. "Read that."

He did, his eyes widening. *Victim was strung up on mile post 101.* It made him want to read the rest, so he scanned it all, not finding anything else. She was right, it was pretty bare.

"What do you think? To me, that sounds like it could be a match."

He nodded and flipped the page. "The report's pretty flimsy."

"Yeah. Not only that, but some hapless local cop must've come and taken the body down before they had a chance to photograph it or check for forensic evidence. So it's a classic case of what not to do as a police department. But it's a lead. And I think it means we're dealing with a serial killer."

"Okay . . .," he said, still wiping his eyes. "But even so. This happened a year ago. We'll still need to wait until he strikes again."

"Maybe. But I want to see the crime scene. Maybe we can poke around and ask the local police there what they remember," she said, gathering her things out of her suitcase. "I'm going to take a shower. I'll meet you outside in fifteen?"

Wait. Wasn't it the middle of the night? Confused, he reached behind him and pushed aside the vertical blinds. Yep. Still dark. "It's still night."

She held up her phone. "It's four-thirty. The sun'll be up by the time we get down to this Boles place. Come on. We have no time to lose."

He yawned and stood. As much as he wanted to get back to the bikini girl, he figured that she, like all the women in his life, was gone forever. So he had nothing left to do but fish in his pockets for the key to his room. "All right. Be back in fifteen."

*

Rylie squinted in the morning sun, which was just coming up as they pulled to mile marker 101, in the town of Boles. She jumped out of the passenger side of the truck and ran to it. Of course, the crime had happened almost a year ago. There was nothing to see.

"What, exactly, were you hoping to find?" Brisbane asked, coming up behind her.

"Shh," she said, turning in a slow circle. "I'm trying to see . . ."

He shoved his hands into the pockets of his slacks. "You hoping to get psychic vibes?"

She glared at him. "No. But I thought there could be a clue."

"It happened months ago—"

"I know. But there could've been something about this location that was similar to where Darla McCrea was found. Something that made the killer choose these mileposts out of all the others."

He squinted. "Well, they're both odd numbers."

She turned to him, trying to gauge if he was serious. "And?"

"Sixty-seven. One-oh-one. Yeah." He scratched his chin and pointed to the sign up a little farther, that said Route 86.

"So . . . what are you saying? The guy's a math geek? That's stupid."

Brisbane shrugged. "Yeah, it might be stupid. But right now, other than that one footnote in that crappy report that said the victim was 'strung up on a milepost,' it looks like the only connection we have."

A flimsy one, for sure. But he was right. She'd brought along the file for Nancy Sharpe and scoured it on the ride there, but there was very little information. It could've simply been a coincidence. So there really was no evidence that this was a serial killing, or that whoever murdered Darla McCrea would strike again. That meant that this crime, along with the dozens of others committed along this length of road, was destined to go on the books as unsolved.

Her gut wrenched at the thought.

She stalked over to the milepost and inspected it. It looked new, shiny, as if it'd recently been replaced. "Dammit!" she cried suddenly, clenching her hands into fists. "Why did those idiot cops not do their job? If they'd handled this correctly, maybe we'd have something to go on."

"Maybe," Brisbane agreed, moving slightly to allow her to pace up and down the shoulder. She always paced when she needed to think, and she didn't want anyone in her way. It was nice to know he was starting to understand that about her.

"They're such *idiots*," she grumbled to no one in particular.

"Yeah, well, you might want to keep the idiot talk to a minimum because here comes one of them now."

She looked up. Sure enough, a squad car was pulling to the shoulder behind them. She watched the man who stepped out, already judging him harshly, though he didn't look like the raving moron she'd accused him of being. He was well-dressed, trim, and even handsome, for an older, fifty-something man, wearing the uniform of the Wyoming Highway Patrol. He looked over the truck and called to them, "Can I call you a tow?"

Brisbane flashed his badge. "No, officer. We're with the FBI. Investigating a couple of murders that happened earlier and trying to see if there's any connection. Do you know of a body that was found in this area?"

He nodded. "You're talking about the case of that prostitute. Yeah. I know it."

"You do?" Rylie moved forward. "Are you the one who took the body down before any real investigation could be done?"

Next to her, Brisbane stiffened. The officer—Officer D Harvey, from his badge—gazed at her, face falling. "No. That was another officer. But we authorized him to do so. It was a terrible sight. Didn't want anyone driving by to see that."

Rylie scoffed. "What's terrible is that Nancy will never have justice because the investigation was botched."

Harvey gave her a hard look and then addressed Brisbane. "It was terrible. An awful sight."

"You saw it?"

"Yeah. I got here just as they were taking it down. The woman was stretched out, like some kind of sacrifice. Whoever had done it had taken great care in putting the body out like that. Must've been someone really sick. I still have nightmares about it."

Rylie gritted her teeth. The crime was sounding more and more similar to Darla McCrea's murder. "And the report is correct that you had no leads then?"

"No. We thought it was probably some drifter, picked her up, used her, and disposed of her. No sign of sexual abuse—he'd just murdered her." He visibly shuddered. "You saying there was another crime, just like that one?"

Brisbane nodded. "Similar. We're trying to discover whether there's a connection, and as you can imagine, it's a little difficult with the report we have from your office."

Harvey nodded. "Yeah. Our team isn't used to dealing with that kind of thing. So the reporting might not have been the greatest."

Rylie snorted. "You think?"

"Boles is a small, safe community. We haven't had anything like that in years. Of course, with that damn highway going through our town, I suppose it was just a matter of time. That route ain't safe. Hope you catch whoever did it."

"Well, it's a lot harder now, considering," Rylie shook the file in her hand, gripping it so hard in her fist that the pages wrinkled. "I'm surprised you even have a job, with the way you handled things with this case. Because I'm telling you, it's not good."

The officer stared at her, and his lower lip began to tremble.

Brisbane put his hand up and turned to her. "Uh, Rylie? Why don't you wait by the truck while I ask a few more questions?"

"No, I—"

"Wolf. I've got this."

She studied him, ready to argue. Ready to punch something, the rage inside her about to bubble over.

She took a deep breath. He was right. She never said anything she regretted, but right now, she was so incensed, she wasn't thinking clearly. She could jeopardize the investigation the same way that the officers had.

"I'm sorry," she murmured, then skulked off toward the truck, climbed into the cab, and went through the file again. She pulled out a map and started to go through it, looking for a pattern between the two mileposts. They were fifty-two miles apart from one another, in different states. There really wasn't very much else. She twisted the map, following the route over the state line and through the National Forest. The towns were all small, rural, one-horse stops on the road. Most of them were desolate and sparsely populated. That was what all these stops had in common.

A few moments later, the door to the truck opened and Brisbane sat inside, letting out a long sigh.

"Anything?" she asked, her frustration growing as she tried to wrangle the map and fold it.

He took it from her, did a little expert origami, and folded it within seconds. "Yeah. Actually. Officer Harvey said there was another murder, somewhere south of here, that was similar. A couple weeks ago, the police from the town—Crystal Springs—had looked into it, but he didn't think they found much." He pulled back on the cover of his notepad and read. "The victim was named Preston Baker."

"Preston?" She frowned, "A male victim?"

"I would infer that." He started the car. "It goes without saying that you'll want to check it out, right?"

She nodded, trying not to be miffed that by keeping a cool head, he'd uncovered more information than she had. "Right."

CHAPTER FIFTEEN

As they drove south toward the next crime scene, Rylie scoured her files, trying to find more information about this crime. It'd happened six months ago, and yes, involved a twenty-three-year-old young man who was travelling from Montana to his childhood home outside of Rock Springs for a family reunion. He'd called his sister from the road, saying he was about an hour away, and then had disappeared. According to the report, which was a little better, he'd been found strung up against mile post 89.

"Eighty-nine is an odd number," she said, mostly to herself.

"And," Brisbane mumbled. "It's also the year of my birth."

"Well, that's an interesting connection. So there are only five-hundred other odd numbers that might be available to him." She gazed at him. "What else?"

She'd meant it as a joke, but from his frown, he was clearly in no mood to play around. She got it. That meant they were back at square one.

When he spoke next, he exploded slightly, not violently, but as if he'd been holding something in for a long time. "Let me ask you something. Do you intend to make everyone we interrogate hate us?"

"What? I—"

"Like I said, you catch more flies with honey. I was a Navy Seal, Wolf. I can muscle my way in and intimidate someone if I want to. I *don't* want to. Because I've found a better way of getting results."

He was a Navy Seal? Strange, he seemed far too rainbows-and-sunshine for that, the type of guy who liked warm sweaters and hugging puppies. She said, "Your size alone would be intimidating, if you'd just drop the Shirley Temple act. No one is intimidated by little old me. I have to do something to tell them I mean business."

He nodded. "I get it. I guess. I just . . . can you do me a favor? The next time you think you're gonna fly off the handle . . . can you just, not?"

She didn't say anything.

"Because I would've gotten that information from him a lot sooner if you hadn't put him on the defensive."

Her lips twisted. He was probably right.

"Positivity. It's a good thing to have."

She gazed at him, a little astonished. "How can you be? With all these horrible crimes we're investigating? Why are you not more jaded?"

"Because I firmly believe there's still a lot more good in the world." He winked at her.

Wow. He was such a glass-half-full, Forrest Gump-type, if ever she saw one. She had to admit, she was envious. His suit of armor to protect him from this terrible world was impressive. "Okay. Fine. I'll try to be a little nicer."

"Good. Thanks."

The truck sailed past Milepost 89. Rylie's eyes followed it until it disappeared in the rearview mirror. "Weren't you going to stop?"

"Why, so we could look at another cold crime scene with absolutely no clues whatsoever?" he asked, taking the next exit. "I'm doing us even better. Harvey called in and got us an appointment with the coroner in the case. We have a meeting with him at eight."

She raised an eyebrow. She had to admit, that was a pretty good idea, and yes—much better than looking at another milepost. "All right," she muttered, feeling slightly like a third wheel in her own case.

They pulled up to the Crystal Springs medical center, a small, one-story building, and took the elevator down to the coroner's basement office. A receptionist showed them in. The coroner, a stout man with a substantial belly, pressed up against his desk, was busy signing documents. He looked up and took off his bifocals, then stood and shook their hands. "FBI agents, huh?" he said, with a deep Southern accent. "I haven't seen many of your kind in these parts."

"I'm sure the Preston Baker case was something you don't see every day, huh?" Rylie asked, trying to be positive, since she promised her partner she would be.

"That's right. I'll never forget it, as long as I live."

They sat down, and Brisbane said, "What was the cause of death?"

"Strangulation," he said matter-of-factly, reaching over and opening a file, which he pushed over to them. "The killer used a rope to strangle the victim, and that same rope was used to tie him to the milepost."

He flipped to another photograph, which showed the man, legs out straight in front of him, head lolling, tied to the post with a sign that said *89.* A bit of the white ligature was visible among bloodied bruises and his long, shaggy hair. Rylie said, “It looks like he was beaten, too?”

“Those injuries are consistent with the crash.”

“Crash?”

“His car was found two miles from this site, smashed against a tree. Someone in the backseat of the car wrapped the rope around his neck while he was driving. There were skid marks all over the road, I’m told.”

Rylie read a paragraph from the police report:

Victim’s car was found near MM 166. Subject of recent motor vehicle accident, airbags deployed. The cashier working at the Sunoco Station, at the Pooler Exit, at MM 165 said she served the victim. Likely, the assailant gained access to the car when the victim went inside the store to pay for his gas.

She read the rest of the report, but there was nothing much else. “Was there any evidence on the body? DNA? Anything that could help identify the body?”

“No. It was clean.”

“And did the gas station he stopped at have outdoor security cameras to catch the guy getting into the back of the victim’s car?”

The man shook his head.

Rylie smacked her hand on the desk. “Well, that’s just great. We have absolutely zero to go on, now.”

Next to her, Brisbane bristled. She took in a deep, breath, trying to calm herself.

“I’ll tell you this, though,” he said, lacing his hands together. “Whoever did it took a lot of care with the body. Making sure it was just so. I don’t know if you can tell that from the photograph. I’ve seen a few dead bodies in my life, but there was something—I don’t know. Too perfect about it. The way the limbs were stretched out. The way the clothes were on the body. It seemed almost posed. You know?”

Rylie swallowed the bitter taste in her mouth. Darla McCrea’s body had looked the same.

“You said that the victim’s family lives around here, in Hot Springs?” Brisbane asked, studying the photographs. “Do you have an address? I think we should probably talk to them.”

The coroner scribbled something on a pad and handed the paper to them. “This here is his brother’s place. I guess his parents passed away a few years ago.”

"Great, thanks!" Rylie said, trying to be positive as she took the paper and glanced at it. *Blake Baker, 42 Willow Way, Hot Springs, AR.* "That's super."

The coroner looked at her like she had something crawling out of her nose. And as they left, Brisbane looked over at her. "Super?"

She shrugged. "Yeah. I'm trying to be positive, like you said."

He shook his head. "Okay. But you don't have to overdo it."

*

Blake Baker lived in a modest rancher just outside the town of Hot Springs. There were bikes outside and an old swing set in the backyard, plus a couple of old cars, up on blocks, in the front. As they pulled up onto the gravel drive, Rylie said, "I'll let you speak first, Mr. Charming, so you can pour on the honey and catch those flies."

He didn't argue. They walked to the front screen door and a large dog started to bark at them even before he rapped. A little boy came to the door and nudge the dog away. "Who are you?" he asked, awed.

"I'm Michael Brisbane from the FBI, and this is my partner, Rylie Wolf."

Brisbane flashed his badge, and the kid's eyes widened. "Wow! You want to talk to my dad?"

"If it wouldn't be too much trouble. Is he home?"

A man came down the hallway, then, finishing with his tie. He was wearing a white shirt and his hair was slicked back as if he'd just gotten out of the shower. "FBI?" He looked confused. "Is this about my brother?"

Brisbane nodded.

"Has something changed in the case?"

"No. Not exactly. Can we talk to you for a few moments about it?"

He nodded, then motioned them outside. "I'd rather not let the kids hear anything about what happened," he said in a low voice, leading them out to the driveway. "I'm a little late for my job at Kroger's. What can I help you with?"

"We'd like to know a little about your brother," Rylie put in, unable to keep herself quiet. "He was on his way home?"

Blake nodded. "He was. For the weekend. He lived and worked up in Billings but we always have a family reunion. So he was going to come down for that. He was working a later shift so he said he'd be in late. Called me around ten o'clock from a place where he'd stopped to get gasoline and told me he would be here in another hour. I waited up for him, but he never came. Next thing I knew, the police were knocking on my door."

"Did he sound normal when he spoke to you?" Rylie asked.

He nodded. "A little tired. But he'd just worked a full shift at the auto parts store in Billings, so I guess that made sense. He said he was looking forward to crashing in our guest room and didn't want to be woken up until the reunion."

"He didn't mention anything strange that had happened on the road? Someone following him?"

Blake shook his head. "Nothing. Though Preston was always a little oblivious about those things. My little brother wasn't the most of observant of people. If he had been, maybe he would've noticed that man sneaking into his car at the gas station." He checked his watch. "I'm sorry. I'm late as it is. If you want to ask more, my wife's inside. She'll make you coffee?"

Rylie shook her head. "No. I think we're done here."

They went back to the truck, and it was only when Brisbane was backing out of the driveway that she smacked her hands on her thighs. "None of this is helpful at all."

"What are you talking about? We've all but confirmed these murders are the product of the same guy."

"But we don't have any concrete evidence. No definite connection," she said, gnawing on her lip. "The only thing they have in common is that they were out on the highway, at night. That's it."

Brisbane opened his mouth to say something, just as a call came through on the car. He pressed a button on the dashboard. "Brisbane here."

"Hey, Agent. This is Wally Sparks, from the Montana Highway Patrol."

"Oh, hey, Sparks. How are you doing this morning?" Brisbane said brightly. Rylie rolled her eyes. Why did it already seem like he was best friends with these people?

"Good, good," he said, but then his tone turned somber. "Listen, I'm here at Fort Winston, on the Montana-Wyoming border, and I think you should come up here. I think we have a bit of a situation you might be interested in."

"Oh yeah?" he asked, turning up the volume. "What's that?"

"I think we have another one."

CHAPTER SIXTEEN

Rylie practically jumped out of the truck, as soon as they arrived near milepost eighty, which was right on the border, before the Wyoming state line.

Milepost Eighty-three. Another odd number.

But definitely the most promising crime scene yet. Because for this one, she didn't have to rely on witness accounts, or photographs. This one, she could actually see with her own two eyes.

"Hey, wait, are you sure you want to--" Brisbane called after her, but she was already past the hood of his truck, heading toward the small gathering of police officers.

"Of course I do!" she called back as she approached the crowd. Nudging the officers aside, she came upon the victim. The moment she broke through, she wasn't so sure.

Bile gurgled in the back her throat, and she felt dizzy and nauseated. The pretty blonde woman was spread out, much like the other victims in the pictures she'd seen. Her pale skin was bruised along the neck, where the ligature affixed her to the pole. Her blonde curls were spread out nicely around her shoulders, and her legs were splayed in front of her. She was wearing white nurse's shoes and a fuzzy pink cardigan, stained with brown spots that might have been coffee, that had a nameplate on it: TONYA BIRCH, RN. She'd been set up, just as the others had been.

Next to her, Brisbane let out a groan that emanated deep from within his throat. "Dammit," he said. "Who is she?"

At that moment, Rylie's eyes lost focus on everything but the body in front of her. Everything else seemed to blur around her. The woman could've been alive, asleep, the way she was lying there, but the ligature around her throat told a different story. She'd been strung up like a scarecrow.

Sounds faded to a low buzz, kind of like a record player on too slow a speed. She heard a voice, the voice of Montana Highway Patrol officer Wally Sparks, say, "Her name is Tonya Birch. We found that much out because she left her purse in her car. We located that about a mile down the road, on the shoulder. Looks like the killer was in the back of her car, strangled her there. We found blood and signs of a struggle in there. But we don't think she died until he brought her out here."

Rylie frowned. Hadn't anyone ever told her that age-old bit of advice? It was rule number one, when women went traveling alone. Men, maybe, weren't told that as much, which was why Rylie understood poor Preston Baker getting it. But Tonya? Maybe she'd been busy. Or maybe she'd simply forgotten.

A truck rumbled by, sending a gust of wind at her back that nearly knocked her over, stirring her from her thoughts.

Rylie crouched down in front of the body. "Cause of death was strangulation?"

He nodded. "Seems like it. I'm sure the coroner will say so."

She touched her hands to the ground and noted the ruts in it. Yes, she'd definitely been fighting, here. Out here, in the open, where anyone could've driven by and seen her, taking her last breath.

The only problem was that no one had. This highway was too remote. Too desolate.

She let out a sigh and stared at the mile-marker. 83.

Taking out her phone, she typed into the notes section: 61, 83, 101, 97.

She stared at the numbers until Brisbane appeared over her shoulder. "I've been staring at those damn numbers for a while, now. If you can find a connection among them, you're a better person than I am."

"It's not even like he's going in a definite direction," she said with a frustrated moan. "He's going up and down the corridor."

"I think he's doing that on purpose, so we have no idea where he's going to strike next," Michael said, turning away from the gruesome sight. "But the good thing is, we know he's probably going to strike again. That it's a serial killing."

"But he's speeding up, Michael," she said with a shake of her head. "Preston Baker a week ago, then Darla McCrea two days ago, and now Tonya Birch. He's definitely speeding up." She shuddered. "I wonder why?"

"Who knows? Maybe because he's getting braver, since he thinks he can't be caught. But that means he'll get careless. And we'll stop him."

She nodded, hoping that was true. "What do we do now?"

She expected him to say something about how it was time for breakfast, but to her relief, he said, "Let's go back to police headquarters. We can sit down and compare the cases."

Rylie nodded. "Sounds like a plan."

*

Brisbane's mind wasn't totally on the case, because he did stop in at a Bob Evans and get breakfast sandwiches and coffee. She didn't mind—she needed the coffee to stay awake, since she hadn't slept at all the night before.

At the State Highway Patrol headquarters in Fort Winston, on the Montana-Wyoming border, they sat opposite each other in one of the interrogation rooms, pouring over facts and files from the case. It was all stuff she had read before, but she kept reading it again and again, thinking she must've missed something. By the time she finished her second coffee, she was out of steam.

"I haven't found anything. Have you?"

Brisbane, who was hunched over the table, his chin on his hand, shook his head. Then he sat back, stretched his long arms over his head, and yawned. "Zero."

Just then, the door opened, and Officer Sparks poked his head in. "Agents, Tonya Birch's sister just came in to ID the body and pick up some of her belongings. Did you want to talk to her?"

Rylie nodded and pushed away from the table. "Did forensics finish with the car?" she asked the officer as they walked down the hall.

Sparks nodded. "Yep. Nothing. The killer didn't leave much behind at all. They're having a few prints and hair analyzed, but they think it all belongs to the victim."

Rylie sighed. Of course.

When they reached the front lobby, they found a young girl of about twenty-one, sitting in the waiting area, her eyes rimmed in red. There was a tall boy sitting next to her, his arm around her.

"Hi, are you Tonya Birch's sister?" Rylie asked.

She nodded. "I'm Kelsey. This is my boyfriend, Brock."

Rylie shook their hands, and Brisbane did the same. "Kelsey, do you mind if I ask you some questions?" she said.

"N-no," she stammered.

"Where do you live?"

"I live in Cheyenne. I go to school at the University of Wyoming. But my sister was a travel nurse. She lived in Stuttgart. Outside the city."

"She lived alone?"

"No. She had a roommate. I forget her name. I only met her once."

"Husband or boyfriend?"

"No. She was single."

"When was the last time you spoke to her?"

"I spoke to her yesterday morning. She was going to work—she'd gotten a job working at the hospital in Billings, Montana, and then she was going to be back this morning. We were supposed to go out to the spa together. She always gets run ragged when she travels—so she needs the spa to recuperate." She glanced at her boyfriend and let out an anguished sob. "I can't believe she's gone. Who could've done this to her?"

"That's what we're trying to find out," Brisbane said kindly, reaching out and touching her shoulder.

Rylie nodded. "I know this is hard. But we appreciate any information you can give us—even the smallest thing might be the clue to helping us find this killer. Did she ever mention to you being followed, or tell you that she saw anyone strange while she was up in Billings?"

Kelsey frowned. "No. She didn't. All she did was talk about her job and how she couldn't wait to get home. That's it."

"It looks like she made a stop, which was where the suspect entered her car."

Kelsey nodded. "Which makes no sense. I can't believe she'd ever stop, and there, at that donut shop, of all places."

"Why?" Rylie asked.

"Well, she's used to traveling at night. But she worries. She knows how to be safe. That's why I can't believe that this happened. She used to tell me that she would always fill up and make sure she had enough gas before she left the hospital because she hated stopping at any of those roadside places. Especially on the Highway Thru Hell."

Rylie looked up, "She knew of this highway's reputation?"

The boyfriend, Brock, let out a low laugh. "Uh, everyone in the state knows about the highway's reputation. We all try to avoid it. I know some people who drive hundreds of miles out of the way so they won't come across it."

"But Tonya couldn't," Kelsey explained. "It's the fastest way up to Billings from her place."

Rylie looked at Brisbane, who seemed to have nothing more. She said, "Well, thank you for your time."

She walked away from them and looked at her partner. "Well, that's no help," she whispered. "A kid who worked at an auto parts store, a prostitute, a fifty-four-year-old homemaker, and a traveling nurse. There's no connection between these victims. They're completely different in every way, except for being in the wrong place at the wrong time."

"Yeah. I know. But there's got to be some connection." He snapped his fingers. "I'm going to call Beeker. Maybe he can run the milepost numbers through the computer and see if it spits out anything."

After everything, they should've had more. They had a fresh crime scene, and she'd hoped, with that, the answers would become crystal clear. But there were no answers, unless the forensic data revealed something. They still had so little to go on.

And the killer had only waited a couple days between the most recent murders. If they wanted to stop him from killing again, they'd have to act fast.

She shrugged and followed her partner into the back room. "I guess. That's better than nothing."

CHAPTER SEVENTEEN

Fifteen minutes later, Rylie Wolf stood in front of the bulletin board in the conference room with Michael, staring at the four pushpins that they'd placed on a giant map of the area. The resulting shape wasn't even a quadrilateral—it was a strange, flattened, open-ended line that appeared to be going nowhere along the route.

"And this tells us . . . what?" Brisbane said, dragging a hand down his face. It wasn't even noon, yet, and he already had a five o'clock shadow.

"It tells us that we're going nowhere," Rylie grumbled, sipping a new cup of coffee. This one, from the police station, was terrible; but right now, she needed all the help she could get.

"Hey. Positive. Remember?" he said to her. "There's something here. I can feel it."

"And what about this mishmash of nothing tells you that?"

"Maybe nothing here. But the fact is, we know they're connected now. There's something very ritualistic about the killings and the presentation of the body. It's planned. I don't for one second think he picked these people up randomly, because he had the opportunity. So we just have to figure out what it is that ties them all together."

"Hey, look at this," Beeker said from behind his computer.

They turned. The guy with the shock of red hair was doing exactly what Rylie had seen him do, every moment since she'd met him—typing like crazy and staring into his computer screen. They gathered around the computer screen to find a very high-tech mapping system.

"Very few maps are visually accurate, because they're drawn to scale," he said, finally stopping and looking at Rylie. "Like if you think about it, every map of America shows Alaska as about the same size as Texas, when in reality it's more than twice its size."

Brisbane nodded. "So what are you saying?"

"So if you're looking for a pretty little pattern on that map with the four points you have, you're not going to see much. This map is a little more accurate."

They looked at it. “Okay, okay,” Rylie said, leaning in. “So if we go by this, he’s kind of making a bit of loop. So if he’s going to go South again, there’s a good chance he’ll strike somewhere between these two mileposts?”

Brisbane shook his head. “There’s no saying he will go south. Yeah, he’s zigzagged so far, but we only have four murders to go on. That isn’t enough to form much of a guess on.”

“Right. But if we don’t do something, someone might be dead tonight,” Rylie said, hands on her hips. She looked over at Wally Sparks. “I propose we notify all precincts along the highway and ask them to put extra patrols on, all the way from here to Hot Springs.”

Sparks choked, “That’s a long stretch of road, ma’am.”

Brisbane nodded. “Many of these police departments only have one or two guys on at night. That’s a lot to ask.”

Sparks added, “Not to mention that while I might be able to round up the police precincts in Montana, I don’t never talk with the ones over the state line.”

“Well, we should ask them to put out whatever they can spare,” she said, scanning their faces. They still looked doubtful. So much for her partner, backing her up on this. She didn’t want to resort to pulling rank, but he left her no choice. “As the only former BAU agent here, I’m going to have to insist—”

“I’m BAU, too,” he said.

She froze. “What?”

He nodded. But it couldn’t be true. If he’d been in the same unit she’d been in, wouldn’t a *Hey, me too!* have been in order? What was he playing at?

“I thought you said . . .”

“I didn’t say anything,” he said, looking away.

That was true. He hadn’t. One of the only things she’d told him about herself was that she was BAU, and though he’d talked incessantly about himself, he hadn’t said anything about that. “Why is that?” she wondered aloud.

Still not looking at her, he squinted at the map. Okay. Something told her she’d hit upon a nerve. She stared at him, suspicious, for the first time. “Well, I still think that we should put extra patrols on that stretch of road if we can manage it.”

Brisbane shook his head. “If we’re wrong, it won’t matter how many people we put on the road. Someone else might die tonight.”

"But at least we will have done something," Rylie insisted, rubbing her eyes.

"Guys," Beeker said suddenly. "You don't need to put all those patrols out. Look at this."

They leaned in.

"This, here, is a program I've been developing and testing. Based on the longitude and latitude of the coordinates you give me, it can determine, with almost eighty percent accuracy, the likelihood of where a criminal might strike again," he said proudly, tilting the screen so they could see. "And based on the data I inputted, we've got two locations that it's giving a *high probability* for. Here, and over here."

Rylie squinted. One of them was Milepost 67 in Wyoming, and the other was Milepost 73, which, if she remembered correctly, was only a few miles from where they stood.

"Now, that's what I'm talking about," Brisbane said with a satisfied nod, ruffling the kid's red hair as if he was his little brother. "Good job, Beek. I think it's seventy-three."

She stared at him. "Why?"

"Because look. If this was the last murder, then this is closer. So it makes sense," he explained, pointing.

"But you yourself said the murderer was zig-zagging, and that means it's probably 67," she said, nodding with certainty.

He rolled his eyes. "Wanna bet?"

"No. I just know. So that's where I'm going to be tonight. If my partner wants to go split up and go elsewhere, fine by me." She held up her chin like she didn't need him.

He snorted and looked at Sparks. "Looks like we're going to be at 67," he said, running a hand through his hair. "You think you guys can have an unmarked car on seventy-three?"

Sparks nodded, "Will do."

Then he looked at Rylie in a way that said, *You owe me.* "I sure hope you're right. Otherwise . . ."

"Be positive," she said with a small smirk, but deep down, she was hoping so, too.

CHAPTER EIGHTEEN

A cold wind blew through the desolate wasteland that was this area of Wyoming, rocking the pick-up. Rylie wrapped her hands around a mug of tepid, bitter coffee and took a sip.

"I sure hope you're right," Brisbane said next to her. *Again.* He'd said it three times in the last hour, and every time he did, she felt less and less sure.

"And I sure hope you're not a total ass."

He looked at her. "What does that mean?"

"It means, would you stop saying that?" she grumbled, checking in the rear-view mirror. They were stationed behind some bushes, and though the other officers in the dragnet weren't visible, she knew they were out there. They'd stationed officers in hiding at the two exits on either side of milepost 67, and were now parked off the road on the highway, between them, waiting for any sign of trouble. "If I'm wrong, I'm wrong, but I just had a hunch. Call it women's intuition."

"Uh-huh," he said, running his hands through his dark hair.

"Besides, Sparks put a detail on seventy-three."

He had, just in case. But they all knew it couldn't do much. The force had been spread thin as it was, so Sparks putting one guy at the exit before the number seventy-three milepost probably wouldn't do much. "Uh-huh." He picked up the radio receiver, "Sparks. You there?"

"Yep," Sparks was at the Fort Winston exit, and another crew of younger officers was at the Pinedale exit. "No sign of anything."

"You hear from the others?"

"Yep. All quiet."

She checked her phone. It was after midnight. Maybe this was not the killer's night. Maybe he'd decided to take the night off.

Gritting her teeth, she willed something to happen. No, of course, she didn't want any more murders, but she wanted this guy to be caught.

Also, and maybe even more desperately, she wanted to be right. To look at Brisbane and say, *Ha. I told you so.*

She shook her head to get rid of that thought. What was she, twelve? But she really did want to prove herself, to show them, just in case they were thinking that she'd been sent all the way out here because no one wanted her in Seattle, that she was useful.

Just then, headlights slashed across her line of vision, and a car seemed to slow down.

"Look," she said, nudging Brisbane as the car pulled to the road by mile-marker 67.

Brisbane sat up and moved to the edge of his seat as the car cut its engine. It looked to be an old, boxy sedan, maybe a Toyota Camry or a Honda Accord. A figure hopped out, too large to be a woman, and trudged toward the trunk.

Rylie held her breath as Brisbane said, "This could be him." He took a breath and spoke into the receiver. "Sparks, we're seeing a man stopping here at mile 67. He's going through his trunk."

"Hell," Sparks replied. "We didn't see anyone here. You think he already got someone, early on?"

The figure worked in the darkness, doing something at the trunk, facing away from them. Rylie couldn't stand the suspense. She pushed open her door.

"Wait, where are you going?" Brisbane asked.

"I've got to see . . .," she said, slowly closing the door so it barely made a thud. Hand on the butt of her gun, she crept softly up the embankment, toward the trunk of the car.

Brisbane followed her. "Don't do anything stupid."

Who, me? she mouthed to the wind, moving slowly and silently forward.

When she reached level ground, she leveled her gun at the man. "FBI! Show me your hands!"

The man froze and let out a wail, then lifted his hands.

Brisbane let out a sigh and shone his flashlight toward a skinny man in jeans and a t-shirt. "I thought I said not to do anything stupid," he mumbled under his breath to her, coming up to the man with his own gun raised. He called, "Turn around. Slow."

The man turned. He blinked in the brightness of the light, his face frozen in shock. "I'm sorry!" he cried, again and again. "I didn't know I couldn't stop here!"

"Why did you stop?" Rylie asked, coming close and peering in the trunk. She moved things around, looking for the body. Instead, she found a duffel, a sleeping bag, and a spare tire.

He twirled something on his finger. It looked like a deflated balloon. "I was getting this for my wife. She's nine months pregnant and she wasn't very comfortable."

Brisbane squinted. "What is it?"

"It's a blow-up chair pad," he explained, holding it up for their inspection.

A sinking feeling growing in Rylie's gut, she shifted to the side and saw a woman, sitting in the front passenger's seat, looking terrified.

A cold wind blew, and she holstered her gun, and hugged herself, then looked up and down the barren highway for something she might have missed. But there was nothing. She let out a sigh. "Oh. We're sorry. We were looking for someone else."

"You can go," Brisbane said, waving him on.

He didn't have to be asked twice. He jumped in his car and sped off onto the highway.

Then he looked at Rylie, who did her best to avoid his disappointed glare. Before he could say words of *I told you so,* she marched back to the car so she didn't have to hear it.

When he was back inside, she turned the heater up to blow on her cold cheeks. "I really thought this was it," she murmured. "I'm sorry."

He shrugged. "Not a big deal. We all make mistakes. I've made more than my share."

She stared at him, a little surprised by that reaction He could've rubbed this in her face, but he hadn't. It made her feel worse for getting down on him, for wanting to be the one to tell him *I told you so*. "Thanks." She gnawed on her lip. "You know. Maybe you were right about the other exit. Seventy-three."

He checked his phone and sighed. "You heard Sparks. The other detail there didn't see anything. But it's getting late."

She shook her head. "I felt for sure he'd try something tonight. Maybe we should go there?"

"I don't know—"

Just then, the radio crackled, and a voice came on. It was Wally Sparks. "Hey, Agent Brisbane?"

"I'm here. Over."

"Yeah . . . a little bit of a problem with the detail on seventy-three. That's Cobbs. He's a new officer. Only been on the force two months."

Rylie leaned forward. "What problem?"

"Well, he hasn't answered my last two calls. I'm starting to get worried," Sparks said.

Brisbane started the engine on his truck. "We're on it," he said, pulling onto the road. "We'll call you and let you know what we've found once we get there."

He swerved out onto the road, heading to the turnaround in the median. When he got there, he carefully came to a stop and made the U-turn to head west on the road. Meanwhile, Rylie's heartrate rocketed, but she bit her tongue to keep herself from complaining about his grandfatherly driving skills.

After all, Cobb was there, at 73, alone, because she'd made the call.

What if something terrible had happened to him? What if the killer had gotten to him and now he was dead?

*

When they arrived at the number 73 milepost, they pulled to the side of the road. Rylie quickly hopped out and used the flashlight on her phone to scan the area, looking for the police car.

She saw it, by the tree-line, hidden by shadows. Meanwhile, the wind blew fiercely, whistling through the air as she broke into a run, her cheeks pummeled by the force of it.

She skidded to a stop when a man said, in a tremulous voice, "Freeze. Don't come any closer."

She squinted as her flashlight illuminated the figure of a small, lanky man in a uniform similar to Wally Sparks's. He was standing near the police cruiser and had his gun pointed at her and was blinking in the bright light.

"Cobb?" she asked as Brisbane joined her.

"Yeah?" He sounded like a scared little kid. "Who are you?"

"It's Agent Brisbane and Agent Wolf, from the FBI," she said, letting out a sigh of relief. "Are you okay?"

"Uh, yeah," he said, lowering his weapon. "What are you guys doing here?"

"We came for you," Brisbane said, out of breath. "What the hell? Why didn't you respond to Sparks on the radio?"

"Oh," he said sheepishly, hanging his head. "I would've. But I was sitting there, drinking coffee, and I had to take a leak. I did, in the woods, and then when I came back, I realized I'd locked my keys in the car. I couldn't get back in."

Ryle exchanged a look with Brisbane and grumbled a curse laced with relief, under her breath.

He nodded, "Sorry."

"It's okay, it's okay, kid," Brisbane said calmly, giving the kid a pat on the shoulder. "We're just glad you're okay. We'd thought something happened to you."

He shook his head. "Yeah. I ain't seen anything here. It's dead as hell. And so frigging cold, I'm about to become an icicle."

It was cold, and getting colder. Her hands were already starting to freeze, and the wind was unrelenting. Rylie began to jog back to the pick-up. "I'll radio Sparks and have him send someone to help you out," she said.

When they were back in the cab of the pick-up, she did just that, and by then, it was after 1:30. She let out a sigh. "You think we should call it a night?"

He nodded. "Don't know what else we can do, except sleep here."

He picked up the radio receiver and started to pull away from the road at a more leisurely pace when a call started to come in on his speaker. He pressed a button on the dashboard. "Hey, Beeker. What's up?"

"Not much."

"Yeah, not much with us, either."

"Hey. Yeah. About that, I wanted to tell you something."

"That the program you're developing is a piece of shit?"

"Uh, no. Actually, it's a funny thing," he said, speaking a mile-a-minute. "The coordinates I gave you might not be accurate. My GPS had an old version of the map from that stretch of highway. Highway eighty-six was under construction a couple years ago, and they made changes to the route."

Brisbane listened, confusion dawning on his face. "They did? All right. So what are you saying, Beek?"

"I'm saying that you're probably at new 67. And really, where you need to be is at *old* 67."

"Old 67?" He and Rylie traded glances. "And are you going to tell us where that is?"

"Yeah. You'll have to take the first exit you come to before the milepost, but then you hang a right. Then you should see a sign for it. But I'm warning you, the road's not used anymore. It's probably in disrepair. So be careful."

"All right, Beek, heading there now," he said, disconnecting the call. Then he looked at her. "You might be right, after all."

Maybe. But it didn't matter. They'd still be in the wrong place. So even if she had been right about the number, she knew they were likely too late.

"Go fast," she urged him, and for once, probably because he realized it too, he did.

CHAPTER NINETEEN

Rylie drummed her fingers on her thighs, willing the car to go faster, as they tore into the darkness. This part of northwestern Wyoming was nothing but desolate landscape. Though they drove on for miles and miles, they passed only one set of headlights on the main highway, eighty-six, headed in the opposite direction.

And it became even more desolate when they found the old eighty-six, made up of broken asphalt and covered in dried leaves. Brisbane slowed his truck down only slightly as they drove along it. The mile markers here were barely visible, some missing entirely, others swallowed up by overgrown grass along the shoulder.

"I have a really bad feeling about this," Brisbane said.

Rylie did, too. She wasn't sure if her partner was referring to the beating his new truck was taking, bouncing through the ruts and potholes on the road's surface, or if he meant the murder, but Rylie knew what he meant. Something about this just felt wrong. As if they were being toyed with.

"It's almost as if the killer wanted us to be running around like chickens with our heads cut off," Rylie said as she searched the darkness outside. The headlights illuminated a sign for The Wagon Wheel Inn and Restaurant, which, judging from the boards over the windows, hadn't been in operation for years.

"Yeah. I'm getting that feeling, too." He shrugged as he squinted in the dark. "And you know what? At this point, I'd be just fine with that."

"You would?"

"Yeah. Because if he's busy playing with us, he might not have time to find another victim. And I really don't want to find another body."

"Amen," Rylie said, peering through the window. A thick fog was settling in, clinging to the windshield, making it even harder to see. She leaned forward and wiped at it, realizing most of the condensation was inside the cab of the truck. As Brisbane adjusted the defrost, she looked up and saw the number 67, bent at an odd angle and half-covered by growth. "There!"

He jammed on his brakes. Then he carefully navigated to the side of the road. "You saw something?"

"I saw the milepost. It's back there."

He looked over his shoulder. "Was there . . .?"

She knew what he was getting at. "I couldn't see. It was covered by grass."

"One way to find out." He took a deep breath and reached for the door handle.

She did the same, steeling herself for the terrible sight. It took a few moments to find the post, from its buried position, but when they did, she let out a sigh of relief, "Nothing."

Absolutely nothing. Rylie shone her flashlight around the area, but it looked as though there'd never been anyone there. The mud on the shoulder had been rutted and marred by Brisbane's truck and their footprints. Other than that, it was completely undisturbed. Brisbane let out a groan. "Beeker's program really is a piece of shit, isn't it?"

Rylie dug her hands into the pockets of her jacket to ward off the cold wind and shrugged. "I don't know. I think based on what we had to go on, it was always a long shot."

"So we call it a night?" he asked, pacing up and down the street, staring out into the blustery night.

She nodded, feeling beaten. It was probably too much to wish this case would be buttoned up in one night, so that she could tell the boys back in Seattle, *Look what I did!* and have them groveling at her feet, begging her to come back. "I guess. We can go back to square one and try to figure out where we went wrong."

Heads down, they retreated to the warmth of the pick-up. Once there, Brisbane made a U-turn and pointed the truck toward headquarters.

*

The traveling nurse had been his greatest accomplishment yet.

He assumed she was a nurse, since she was wearing the comfortable shoes and a little cardigan with a hospital badge on it. Poor thing had probably been working all day, and she'd been tired. Too tired, clearly, to check in the back of her car.

A shame. She'd made his job so easy.

But they usually did.

The police, in their stupidity, had made his job even easier. They were left scrambling, as usual, unable to pull their heads out of their own asses. He'd had all the time in the world to arrange the presentation of the nurse on the milepost. That had afforded him the opportunity to make everything just so.

A masterpiece.

Apparently, though, this one wouldn't be so easy.

He dragged a hand down his face as he drove past the mile marker again. The first time, he'd nearly stopped, until he'd seen the pick-up truck, pulling out from the brush. He'd quickly stepped on thc gas, and the F150 had passed him, a mile up the road.

As it had passed, he'd gotten a look at the man at the wheel and the female in the passenger seat. Not a married couple on vacation. These two were on business. Probably Feds.

Which meant that they were onto him.

And that was just fine.

He welcomed the challenge. After all, all the greats had to perform under pressure. Michelangelo not only had to paint the entire ceiling of the Sistine Chapel on scaffolding, head tilted back, arms raised over his head, but he'd had to listen to the complaints of dust and mess from the cardinals. Rodin had turned heartbreak into some of his greatest works. Picasso's *Guernica* would not have been possible without a horrific German bombing. And Van Gogh's self-portrait wouldn't have been quite the same if he'd kept his ear.

All artists went through hardship, and their art was better for it.

Now, as he carefully navigated toward the milepost once again, he looked all around. Fucking sixty-seven. A very important milepost in his life, indeed. Two days before Christmas, they'd gone to the farm and gotten one of the last trees left in the lot. He could almost feel the slap on his cheek, hard and biting, as if it'd happened yesterday. He'd lost a tooth from that, and had bled all the way home. Downstairs, his family had decorated the Christmas tree, but he'd been too out-of-it to participate, too ill. His cheek had been red and swollen for a week.

It had to be 67. It just had to be.

He glanced in the back seat, at who would be the subject of his latest creation.

What a beautiful specimen. He had all the qualities of a Toulouse-Lautrec—pale skin, facial hair. If only he'd have treated his body like the temple it was, he'd be practically god-like. He'd been easy, as well, so easy, it was almost a dream come true. He definitely wasn't local to this area—probably one of those idiots who'd come up from Colorado. Most locals knew enough not to hitch-hike on 86, the Highway Thru Hell, but not this man. He'd been barefoot, strung out, probably didn't even know what state he was in. All he'd had to do was pull over, offer a ride, and, while the addict dozed in the back seat, make his move.

He didn't even wake when the knife was plunged into his gut. In fact, he'd let out a single breath, and his lips curled into a smile, almost of relief. Almost as if he knew he'd do greater things in death than he'd done in life. It was almost too easy.

Not that he minded. He knew that there were people out there who enjoyed the taking of life, who reveled in watching a body still, taking its last, precious breath. To him, though, it was simply a means to an end.

Great art took sacrifice.

As he sat there in his idling car, he stared at the mile marker. Then he looked around. The agents, or whoever they were, were gone, now, but they'd be back. Maybe even soon.

Leaning over the motionless subject in the back seat, he ran a finger down his pale skin of his cheek, to his beard. He didn't have the time he'd like to devote to this beauty. A definite shame.

You will be my Creation of Adam at the Sistine Chapel, he thought. *Created under the conditions that are not ideal, but a great masterpiece, just the same.*

CHAPTER TWENTY

Still in the pick-up, Rylie rubbed her tired eyes. It was after two-thirty in the morning, now, and even the coffee she'd sucked down was failing to keep her awake. Her eyes closed, and threatened to stay that way, until Brisbane let out a long, loud yawn.

"Boy, I'm beat," he said, echoing what she felt.

"I can't believe we were both wrong," she said.

"Well, I can. I mean, Beeker's an IT genius and all, but let's not forget that two years ago, the FBI found him in his parents' basement, where he'd been playing Call of Duty for three days straight."

Rylie glanced at him. "Really?"

"Yeah. He might be brilliant, but he is still a kid." He chuckled. "So I cut him a little slack."

"I think next time he gives us an idea, he needs to come out on a stakeout with us," she said. "Share in the misery."

"I'm all for that," Brisbane said with a nod. "But I think right now, we should have him buy us breakfast."

Rylie's stomach growled in answer. The dinner they'd had the night before was still swimming inside her gut, making her feel queasy. "It's only two-thirty, and I don't think there are many twenty-four-hour places around here, unless you count gas stations and places that are going to make my stomach feel even worse than it does right now."

He nodded. "Yeah, it takes a special kind of person to live on a highway diet. I don't know how truckers manage it."

They were coming up to the old 67 milepost. As it came up, Rylie glanced over at the opposite side of the road, and her hand stiffened on the door handle.

There was something there. A hulking form, propped up against the milepost. And . . . a sedan, parked on the side of the road, its lights dimmed. There was a slight glow in the front of the car, illuminating a figure behind the wheel, with what looked like shaggy, dark hair.

But in a split second, it was gone, behind her.

She craned her neck to look out the back window, but the small rearview mirror in the back of the truck was fogged over. It was almost like a dream, something that couldn't be believed, something likely the product of wishing and hoping, combined with lack of sleep.

But then again . . .

"Agent," she whispered, stiffening. "I think I saw something. On the milepost."

"What?"

"On the number 67 milepost. There was a car, there, too. We just passed it."

He glanced in his rearview mirror. "I didn't see anyth—"

"Not on this side of the road. On the other side."

"Shit. What did you see?"

"I don't know," she said, her heart jamming itself in her throat. "Turn around."

He swerved into the fast lane. "Yeah. I'm looking for a place."

There weren't many official vehicle turnarounds. Rylie had seen very few in the daylight. She motioned to the median. "Just make the U here."

He squinted. "I can't tell if—"

"Hurry, Agent. There might've been a car there. He might still be there. We might be able to catch the killer in the--"

Letting out a curse, he suddenly swerved into the median. The bump was so intense, the top of her head scraped the ceiling. She held on tight to the door handle as they pitched this way and that over uneven terrain before climbing out onto the westbound side of the highway. Once they were on level ground, Brisbane navigated onto the highway and surged forward, toward the milepost.

Rylie held her breath as the milepost came in view. The first thing she realized is that she'd been wrong—there was no vehicle parked on the shoulder.

Or had there been one there, just recently? Sure enough, the headlights illuminated tire marks. "I could've sworn . . ."

Her voice trailed off as she realized something else. Her eyes hadn't been playing tricks on her. There was something on the milepost.

A body, a man with a beard, strung up, just as all the others had been.

She drew her gun, and Brisbane, following her lead, did the same. She stepped out of the car and ran to the milepost. An hour ago, this body hadn't been here.

Brisbane knelt in front of the body and touched the skin. "Still warm. What did you say you saw? A car?"

“Yeah. A car. And I thought a man with shaggy, dark hair. But . . .”

“That’s not much to go on. Anything else? Think.”

Rylie shook her head, looking around for any sign of life. Then she ran back to the truck. “Let’s go. We can catch him. I’ll drive.”

Brisbane straightened. “Are you kidding? He’s probably long gone by now.”

She scanned the road, to where it disappeared, far in the distance. There weren’t any taillights to be seen at all. He was right.

She opened the door. “I’ll call it in to the state police. Maybe they can find him, if he’s still out there.”

But as she made the call, she knew it was too late. The killer wouldn’t stay out on the highway, now. Even if he’d just been here, ten minutes ago, he was now, likely, long gone. Brisbane kicked the ground and clenched his hands into fists. She slumped against the side of the truck, staring into the black night.

They’d lost him.

CHAPTER TWENTY ONE

It was three in the morning before Wally and the rest of the state police arrived to view the crime scene. Rylie and the others stood around the spectacle, making observations and collecting evidence.

"So Beeker's original thought was right," Rylie said. "It was at one of those two spots his computer program had mentioned."

"That means your original thought was right," Brisbane pointed out.

"And you say you were just here, an hour before?" Wally asked, scratching his head. When they nodded, he asked, "And there was nothing there at that time?"

"Nothing," Brisbane said. "I wonder if he was scouting out the area while we were here, waiting to dump the body."

"He doesn't dump. He places," Rylie said. "It looks far too posed, again."

Wally nodded. "Cobbs said he saw this guy, hitchhiking, when he was getting into his position."

"He did?" Rylie asked.

All eyes turned to the young officer, who nodded. "He walked past me. Didn't see me because I was in position, but it was definitely him. We don't get many hitchhikers around these parts."

"That means he was picked up, killed elsewhere, and brought here. But why? There has to be some significance to the numbers," Rylie said, kneeling in front of the body. "What did Beeker say was the reason why those numbers had come up?"

Brisbane shrugged. "I think it was that they're concentrated around one town. Sheridan. Those were the only two exits left."

"So is it right to assume that the killer might live around there?" Rylie asked. "How many people live in Sheridan? This area isn't very populated. Shouldn't we be able to—"

"Nah." Sparks shook his head. "There's too many drifters around here. People who RV around the national parks. And it's all spread out. There's not much to go on."

"But then we should be able to accurately say that the next one should happen near the other milepost, right?" she asked.

Brisbane said, "You'd think. But so far, it's like we're grasping at straws."

"We have more information, now," Rylie said, pointing to the tire marks. "These tire tracks could have only come from a certain kind of car, right?"

"Yeah. A small sedan. So that doesn't really narrow things down all that much, unfortunately," Wally said.

"What about evidence?" Rylie asked. "He leave anything behind this time?"

"We'll have a few things sent up to the lab, but there's a good chance it's just as clean as last time," Sparks said.

"Not necessarily," Rylie said. "This one might be posed, but it doesn't look like as much care was taken with it, if you know what I mean. He was rushed. He thought someone would come back. So he might've made a mistake."

Brisbane nodded. "Yeah. She's right. He might've been lurking around, waiting for us to be gone."

Wally snorted. "And why did he have to do that? He could've dropped the body off at any milepost on the road. Lord knows, there's hundreds of them."

"They mean something to him. Something important," Rylie breathed.

Brisbane nodded. "I think you're right. We just have to figure out what."

He reached into the victim's flannel shirt and pulled out a wallet. He opened it and pulled out an ID. "Cody Thompson. Local kid. From Clearmont."

"Clearmont?" Rylie asked.

"It's east of here. About twenty miles." He rubbed his chin. "Maybe we can take a ride out there and see if his family knows anything that'll help us."

Rylie nodded and tilted her head to look at the victim. Though he had a beard, beneath it was a handsome, baby-face. He probably wasn't more than twenty. His feet were dirty, his jeans hung so low that the bottom cuffs were fraying and crusted in mud. There were two smaller ruts leading to his final resting place, indicating the body had been dragged. He had a single stab wound in his abdomen.

"Damn shame. What was he doing hitchhiking this road? And without shoes?" Sparks asked.

"I don't think we need to guess about that one," Rylie said, pointing to his arm. The sleeve of his flannel had been rolled up, and his alabaster skin was marred with needle marks.

Sparks shook his head. "Heroin. Damn. He was probably strung out and helpless. That drug's claiming so many of our young people. It's a crying shame."

"Well, that's not what claimed *him*," Rylie said, heading back to the pick-up.

As she sat in the passenger seat, she noticed that the sky was beginning to lighten, another day dawning. Another day, and it felt like they were no closer to having any answers to who this killer was, or how they could possibly catch him.

*

When they arrived back at the State Police Headquarters, someone had bought donuts. Despite Rylie's head telling her that she needed to eat better, part of her just didn't care. She grabbed a chocolate ring and wolfed it down as they headed into the conference room to go over what they already knew.

She rubbed her eyes as she sat at the table, looking over the files of the victims.

"I think this is looking for that needle in the proverbial haystack," Brisbane said, sitting next to her. "If you want to go into the back, there are some cots. You can get some rest?"

She shook her head, not taking her eyes off the photograph of the nurse. "No. I want to keep looking at this."

"I don't know if there's anything there," he said.

"There is something. I think the reason why we haven't been able to find a connection is because it's not one we can see. It's personal to the killer."

He was silent for a moment. "Yeah. Maybe. But if that's the case, you're not going to find the answers in there."

"I don't know. Maybe I can . . ." she said, blinking the bleariness from her eyes.

"Agent Wolf?" a voice said from the door.

She looked up to see a female police officer. "Yes?"

"You have a call from the Seattle Field Office."

Cooper. At least someone from home remembered her. She'd been hoping that he'd get in touch with her. "Great, thanks."

She stood up and went to the phone in the main lobby of the building, thinking about what she'd tell him. He'd probably have ideas, try to solve it for her. Most men were like that—she couldn't have a conversation without them trying to find the solution to her problems. She'd just skirt over it, tell him it was under control, and let it lie.

"Hello, Coop?" she said into the receiver.

"Agent Wolf," a decidedly more unfriendly voice said. "It's Matthews."

Her stomach dropped. She'd hoped the next time she talked to Bill Matthews, she'd have something she could rub in his face. Actually, part of her had been hoping that he'd washed his hands of her completely, and wouldn't be trying to get in touch.

No such luck. "Oh. It's you."

"Yeah, it's me. I thought that when I sent you out there, you'd be able to wrap this up pretty quickly."

She nearly laughed. Quickly? She'd only been gone three days. "I'm making progress. I've—"

"Clearly not enough. I've heard there were two more murders since we sent you out there?" he barked.

"Yes, well. That's true. So far, the killer has evaded us. But we're working with local police. Agent Brisbane and I have it under control."

"Under control?" He snorted, "Doesn't sound like that to me!"

He was yelling, so loud, she had to hold the phone away from her ear. She looked around, hoping no one was listening to the conversation. It was an after-hours skeleton crew, and most of the remaining police officers were busy with their own work.

But then her eyes shifted to the conference room, and through the door, she saw Agent Brisbane, watching her carefully.

Great. Perfect. Just what she needed, to have her partner find out that her former boss hated her guts and thought she was completely inept. Maybe he wasn't her supervisor anymore, but that didn't mean he couldn't still pull the strings to get her fired.

"We're taking care of it. I assure you," she said, trying to keep her voice calm.

"You'd better be. Because I tell you, Wolf, you don't know what strings my father had to pull to keep you on. Your days as an agent were numbered. If he hadn't, out of the goodness of his heart, transferred you to that new unit, you'd be out on the street."

Anger welled up inside her. But it was that same anger, that flying off the handle, that had gotten her sent out here in the first place. She bit her tongue. "I understand," she said stiffly.

"Do you? Because if you ruin this chance, believe me, it's the last one you're going to get. We won't be sticking our necks out for you anymore. Got it?"

"Yes," she said, forcing down all the insults she wanted to shout at him.

"All right. I expect a report tonight. And I want to hear that you have a suspect in mind. You got that? I need progress. You understand?"

God, he was treating her like some dog who needed basic commands. "Yes," she said, her voice weak.

"I didn't hear you."

"Yes!" she bit out, in a near-snarl.

Michael Brisbane's eyes had gone back to the files, but the moment the word erupted from her lips, they looked up at her.

"Thank you very much for your concern," she said sweetly, before placing the phone back on its cradle.

Gritting her teeth, she meandered toward the conference room, thinking about that stupid, insufferable man. He hadn't done anything to save her job. He hated her. It was his father who'd stuck his neck out. And yet Bill Matthews acted like he was such a saint, like she should get down on her knees and kiss his feet? Hell, no.

She would rather quit the force entirely.

Maybe that was what she had to do. Give up this job, what she'd dreamed about being, ever since Maren disappeared. Call it a day, find another line of work, and let go of that foolish dream of ever finding her sister again.

When she reached the doorway, she hovered there, thinking of Maren, standing outside the RV, the last time she'd seen her.

The picture was still in her head when Brisbane said, "You okay?"

"Fine," she said through her clenched jaw, as she headed down the hallway to the ladies' room.

"Hey, where you going, Wolf? Want to head out to Clearmont, now?" he called.

"Sure! Just give me a minute!" she shouted after him, pushing open the bathroom door.

Once there, she locked herself in a stall and let out the loudest cry of frustration she could, so thunderous that it pierced her eardrums and shook the walls around her.

CHAPTER TWENTY TWO

Usually, Rylie could doze in cars. The monotonous movement and warmth of the cabin should've had her nodding off. But she felt wide awake as they drove the route to Clearmont. Every time she passed a mile marker, she imagined a body, strung up to it. Twisting her hands in her lap, she thought about Cooper.

He didn't care about her. None of them did. Bill Matthews had probably only called her just to make sure she knew what a dismal failure her work on this unit had been. It'd probably given him great pleasure to make that call.

She was alone, here, without any friends. Anyone to look after her.

It'd been that way, most of her teenage years. Her father had been estranged, since he never got over the murder of Rylie's mom. Even now, she never got a chance to visit him on his ranch in Montana. She never wanted to go back there, but she wasn't even sure she'd be welcome if she did. Rick Wolf was a hard man to like.

And funny, as much as she'd tried not to, she'd wound up a lot like him.

"You sure you're okay?"

Rylie stirred from her thoughts and found her partner staring at her, concern etched in his features.

"Yes. Of course. Why wouldn't I be?"

"You looked a little . . . uh, tense back there. You know?"

Tense? She'd been a lot tense, but she'd thought she was doing a good job of hiding it. "When?"

"On the phone. When you talked to your people back home."

She shook her head. "They're not my people. And that's really not my home."

"Oh, yeah?" He looked at her, waiting for her to say more.

But she didn't want to. She definitely didn't want to tell him anything about her past. So she said, "My supervisor is a bit of a weak, pathetic, ineffective idiot who only got the job because of nepotism."

His brow raised in surprise, and he whistled. "Don't hold back, there. Tell us how you really feel."

She shrugged. "It's true. Everyone says so."

"Nepotism, huh?"

She nodded. "He never even went to the Academy. And so yes . . . I can't help it. I don't like him. With me, respect is earned. And he hasn't earned it."

"Ah." He rubbed his chin, which by now, was filled with more than a little dark stubble. "Sounds rough."

"I'm sure you don't get along with everyone in your field office in Missoula, do you?"

He shrugged. "Well . . . yeah. They're all good guys and girls. Uh, women. We all get along. Like a family."

She stared at him. He was like a Boy Scout. "And then why did you come out here?"

"You know. New challenge. New scenery." He cleared his throat, "That's all."

She narrowed her eyes, wishing there was something more to it. He had a such a perfect, glass-half-full life, with no trauma whatsoever. She couldn't help but envy it. "So there's no dark secret that brought you all the way out here to the middle of nowhere?" she joked. "I'm disappointed."

He shook his head slowly. "Sorry. So did your ineffective boss kick you out of your field office, or did you leave on your own?"

Wow, way to get right to the heart of it. "It was kind of mutual," she lied. "He was fed up with me, I was fed up with him, and I guess we were making it miserable for everyone there."

He nodded, and she hoped he wouldn't ask her any more questions that she'd have to lie about. But he simply said, "I could see why you'd want to get out. That's got to be brutal."

They wound up in Clearmont, a small town with only a single main drag. There wasn't much more than a gas station and a few fast-food restaurants along that main street, and a few homes, scattered on either side of it. Most of them were trailers, set out on a flat, barren, scrubby landscape. The only scenery for miles was a few chocolate-colored, rolling hills, out in the distance, dotted with steer and other livestock, pressed up against a pale blue sky.

"Here we are," Brisbane said, pulling up to a small but well-kept ranch house, which had its own barn and a paddock for horses.

"Cody lived here?" Rylie asked, inspecting it. It looked nicer than she'd been expecting. When her partner nodded, she added, "They know he was killed, right?"

Brisbane nodded. "Sparks said they were notified this morning."

They went to the door, but before they could even knock, a man with a big moustache and a cowboy hat answered. For a moment, Rylie thought she'd found her dad. But then she saw that his eyes were red-rimmed, still wet with tears.

Rick Wolf didn't cry. Not ever. Not even when he'd gotten the news that their mother had been murdered, and Maren had been kidnapped.

"Mr. Thompson?" Brisbane asked. "Are you Cody's father?"

He nodded and opened the screen door for them. "That's right. You all are FBI?"

Rylie nodded.

"They told me you'd be by."

He let them in and settled them in the living room. Rylie had been brought up on a ranch in Montana, so she was familiar with this kind of life, but the house couldn't have been more different than the small, two-bedroom farmhouse she'd called home. This was a sprawling rancher with granite countertops and a massive stone fireplace. They sat down on comfortable stuffed leather chairs. She noticed several photographs on the mantle, most of a family of four, including a young, blonde kid who looked like he had his entire life in front of him.

She thought of the family photos she had with her parents and Maren. She hadn't seen one of those family photographs in ages, not since before the tragedy. Her father had hidden them all.

Mr. Thompson said, "I'm not sure I can help you two very much, but I'll try. I hadn't seen Cody since last year."

Good, that's fine, Rylie thought, looking around, a shiver trailing down her back. *There's too much déjà vu around here. Let's make this short and sweet.*

"Last year?" Brisbane said, next to her. "What had he been up to, in the meantime? Did you know?"

He shook his head. "He graduated school and was learning the ropes from me, to manage the ranch. But then he fell in with the wrong crowd, and we started fighting all the time. We had words, and he left. I tried finding him, but I just ran against dead ends. Truth be told, I thought something like this might happen. Every time the doorbell rang, I expected to see the police there, telling me Cody was dead."

"I'm sorry," Brisbane said, sympathetic. "It must be really hard."

"Yeah. He's my only son." He hung his head.

"Geez, I'm sorry, man," Brisbane said again, placing a hand on his knee. "Really hard."

Rylie gazed at her partner. She understood sympathy, but did he have to go overboard like that? They had a job to do, and gazing around at this ranch, at this once-happy family home, she couldn't help but want to bolt. She said, too quickly, "When was the last time you saw Cody, did you say?"

"Right after Thanksgiving. We were fighting all the time. He said he was going to go into Bozeman, Montana, and start working at a resort there. Make some money on his own." His lips twisted, "I knew he was using, then. He'd been using since high school. He kept trying to get clean, but it'd only last a short time. When he left, he was clean. I was hoping he'd be okay there. But then his mother had a heart attack. I tried to get in touch with him, but his phone was disconnected. I called all the resorts in Bozeman and couldn't find him. When my wife died, he didn't come to the funeral. To this day, I don't even know if he knew she'd passed."

Brisbane shook his head. "I'm sorry about your wife."

Rylie nodded, thinking about her father, who'd been running the ranch in Montana, all alone, for years. Yes, it had been hard. He probably could've used her help. But she'd run away, and never looked back. And somehow, her father had wanted that. He'd never called her, even on holidays, to see how she was. "So you're here all alone?"

He nodded. "I have some hired hands. And my daughter, Ellie—Cody's older sister— comes up from Cheyenne now and then. She works there as a nurse."

"She didn't happen to see Cody recently, did she?" Rylie asked.

He shook his head. "Doubtful. They never got along."

Rylie stood up, eager for escape, and Brisbane followed suit. "Well, thank you—"

"Oh, this is a picture of your family?" Brisbane said, noticing the photos on the mantle. He hesitated there too long, smiling at the smiling family faces. A queasy feeling tangled Rylie's gut. "Wow. Again, my condolences."

Turning away from it, Rylie headed toward the door, and the others followed. "Thank you. If we have any other questions, we'll be in touch."

Brisbane produced a card, which he handed to Thompson. "If you have any questions at all, give me a call. That's my direct line."

He studied the card, then dropped it in the pocket of his work shirt. "Will do."

Rylie threw open the door and took a deep breath of cold, bracing air. When she reached the door to the truck, she turned around to find her partner gazing at her curiously. "What?"

He shrugged and got in. "Nothing," he said, in a way that meant it was definitely something.

She got in. "What?" This time, her tone was more annoyed.

"Just . . . was it me or did you want to get out of there as quickly as possible?"

She snorted. "It was only because you kept saying you were sorry every two seconds."

"Well . . . poor guy. I mean, he lost his wife. Then his son. That's got to be hard."

"Yeah. You said that."

He studied her. "Wow. Cold."

"No. We just have a case to solve, Agent." She folded her arms over her chest and stared straight ahead. "Can we get out of here, now?"

He mock-saluted her and pulled the car around the circular drive, heading out for the highway. "All right. So, what are you thinking?"

She glared at him.

"About the *case*, I mean."

Oh. Okay. She could talk about that. She paged through her notes and frowned. "I don't know. I'm just confused. You've worked in the BAU, so you know. With four similar murders, they'd be a pattern by now. But I don't see what it is. The locations may be surrounding Sheridan, but they might not be. All the victims are different. A few of them were strangled, but some were stabbed. I can't believe he's just acting completely randomly."

He nodded. "Few killers do that. Something has to be motivating him."

"But what?" She sighed and threw her head back against the seat rest as they came to eighty-six. "And I saw him. I actually saw him. But what can I do with that information? We can't just look for a guy with shaggy brown hair who drives a sedan. That describes a lot of the population. It's so frustrating. I feel like the more we look, the less we have to go on."

"I understand."

Of course he did. Michael Brisbane was nothing if not empathetic.

"So where do we go from here?" she asked.

Just as the words left her mouth, a call came in on his phone. It was from Sparks. Brisbane pressed the button on the dash. "Brisbane. What's up? You find anything new, Sparks?"

"Not really. You?"

"Not much from Thompson's family, unfortunately," he sighed. "We're coming in."

"Good. There's a letter here for Agent Wolf. It looks a little suspicious."

The agents glanced at one another. "Letter? What kind of letter?" she asked.

"You can see it when you come in. It wasn't mailed in. I hope you don't mind, but we took the liberty of opening it and reading it. It's a threat."

"A threat? What does it say?"

"You should come in. We took copies of it and sent it to be analyzed right away. It was dropped off at the front desk, earlier today by a man in a dark hoodie and jeans. We have him on camera. But it's not enough to make a positive ID."

Rylie willed the car to go faster. Did the killer actually mean to get in touch with her? That meant that he knew she was on his case. Had he been watching her?

Unfortunately, her partner was back to staying comfortably under the speed limit. "Pick up the speed, Bris."

"Right," he said, pushing on the gas. "Have you heard anything from any of the other precincts about the other murders?"

Sparks laughed bitterly. "You should know by now that we don't communicate. You're the only other connection we have with the other murders. We wouldn't have even known about most of them without you two looking into it."

"All right. We'll be there in a bit." He ended the call and looked at her. "This could be the big break we're looking for."

A threat. Sparks's words kept going through her mind. She was used to criminals hating her. But she'd never run across one so downright psychotic, one who posed his victims like they were on display and who seemed to commit crimes at random.

"I hope so."

*

Moments later, they pulled up at the State Police headquarters. Rylie ran ahead, eager to get her hands on the letter. When she arrived in the conference room, Beeker was there, still working from his computer, and a file folder was resting in the very center of the table.

He pointed without looking up. "That's the goods you're looking for," he said, typing with one hand. "Tells me this guy is one sick freak."

She walked to the manila folder and carefully slipped it open. Sure enough, there was a photocopy of an envelope there. The envelope was addressed simply:

Female Detective

"How did they know . . .," she began, but Beeker spoke up.

"I asked, too. Apparently, you're the only female investigator around here that has worked on the case."

She'd assumed it was something like that. She pushed aside the photocopy of the envelope and found the copy of the letter. The entire page was covered in a blocky, primitive, scrawl. Some of the lines were so dark, as if written with malice, and it looked like in parts, the pen had ripped through the paper.

She read:

Detective! Why do you want to ruin things? Do you not see what is unfolding before your eyes? Something amazing, something the world will never forget. People may not understand, but I feel like you will. They do not have the eye that you have, nor the heart.

I have always had that power to elevate things beyond the surface level. It's something I was born to do. These gifts were bestowed upon me from birth, and I intend on using them to their fullest. You do understand, don't you?

You may think you know where I will leave my next piece. But that is another one of my gifts—I am not predictable. I am singular, something you have never seen. Something the world has never seen! I promise you that in your wildest dreams you will never be able to guess. Yes, my work here is far from done—I am just getting started. So you will hear from me again, and it is coming sooner than you think. I hope you are enjoying the beauty of it all, Detective. I consider you my biggest fan, and I am grateful that you are here to witness this moment in history. This next one is for you.

X

She stared at it with growing horror, hardly realizing that Brisbane was reading over her shoulder until he spat in disgust, "His next piece? What the hell does he think this is, a chess game?"

"Maybe," she said, her voice only a whisper. She read the line, again and again, *I have always had that power to elevate things beyond the surface level. It's something I was born to do.* "He thinks he's some kind of savior. Some kind of god, I think."

Brisbane let out a grunt. "Yeah. He's completely deluded. And he thinks you're his number one fan."

She shuddered. How did he even pick her out, from among the dozens of officers investigating the murders? Was it because she was a woman? Or was it something else? "Do you think he's been watching us?"

"No clue," Brisbane said, sitting down and scrubbing his hands down his face. "It's possible. I guess anything is possible with this case. And like you said, his method of operation is that he has no method."

"No," she said, still mostly to herself. "I think he does have a method, but it's one he doesn't believe any of us can understand. He feels like he's above us all, but he has a purpose. We just need to find out what it is."

Beeker turned his computer around and showed them some grainy, black-and-white surveillance video. It depicted the bushes outside headquarters, and the double front doors. Then there was a video angle of the lobby, taken from up above.

As they watched, a light-colored sedan pulled into a parking space out front. Then, a slim man in a black hoodie stepped out. He moved at a leisurely pace across the lot.

Then he appeared in the lobby. He stood there for a moment, and his lips moved. Then he took a white envelope out of his pocket, set it on the counter, and strode away. When he left, it was with those long, loping strides, as if he had all the time in the world.

Beeker played it, again and again, on loop.

"What kind of car is that? Can you zoom in?" Brisbane pointed at the screen.

Beeker did, but the camera only captured a small part of rear bumper of the car. "Could be anything."

"Zoom in on the face, would you?" Rylie asked.

He did, but all that was visible was a highly pixelated image. It was no good at all.

"It's almost like he's playing games with us," Brisbane muttered.

That's exactly what it felt like. Clenching the letter in her hand, she scanned to the last sentence. *This next one is for you.*

She hoped to God that wasn't true.

CHAPTER TWENTY THREE

The man slowed to a crawl as he drove past the stout building of the police headquarters, daring them to notice him.

They didn't, of course.

It was prime time at headquarters. Noon. The lot was full of cars, and there were plenty of officers going in and out the front doors. A couple of them were gathered together, laughing, shooting the shit.

He braked, slowing almost to a stop, then considered doing a U right there and waving at the officers outside.

Idiots, every one of them.

He'd even gone in there, dropping off the letter for that Detective, earlier that morning. He'd stepped in and said, "I have a letter for the female detective?"

The fat old granny behind the desk hadn't been able to take the donut out of her face before saying, "Oh, you mean for Agent Rylie Wolf? Just leave it over there on the counter, honey." She'd barely even looked up to see him, so he hadn't had to worry about wearing his hoodie and sunglasses. She probably couldn't describe anything other than the sprinkles on her breakfast.

So he had left the note there. He'd lingered there, in the parking lot, waiting for one of them to read the note and come out.

No such luck.

That was why he'd focused in on the girl. Agent Rylie Wolf.

Rylie Wolf was pretty. Prettier than most law enforcement types were. Feminine, too, even though she tried to hide it with her severe black pantsuit and ponytail. She'd easily make a perfect subject. His heart sped up as he imagined stringing her up, laying her out just so, his piece de resistance.

But not just yet.

She was smart, too. He could tell that. He'd locked eyes with her, on the road, last night, and he'd known. She had the intellect to outsmart him. *She* could bring this all down.

Or, if he could just get her to understand, maybe she'd join him.

He felt like she would.

There was something in the way she'd looked at him, something troubling her. A shared history, perhaps. She'd be sympathetic to his cause. She'd understand what he was trying to do, see that the sacrifice was worth it.

He knew it.

Agent Rylie Wolf.

Pulling into a nearby parking lot, he went to a sub shop and got a turkey and cheese sandwich. Sitting in his car and devouring his lunch, he Googled Agent Rylie Wolf.

The first thing he came across was a listing for an FBI agent out of Seattle.

Interesting. An FBI agent?

Well, this was more than he'd expected. A thrilling turn of events, indeed.

He scrolled through the results, finding more and more information about her. She was a go-getter, and had cracked quite a few cases during her decade on the force. There were pictures of her in uniform, wearing her badge, never smiling. It intrigued him.

Why don't you smile, my little Wolf?

It wasn't until the thirtieth page of results that he came to his answer. It was an old article, from decades ago, but it told him everything he needed to know. The headline was: *Mystery and Tragedy in an RV Campsite.*

He read it, and as he did, the veil over the female agent slowly began to lift. She'd been only ten when her mother had been killed, her older sister kidnapped, during a family vacation. There was a photograph of her, big eyes full of uncertainty. The article said the sister hadn't been found.

Had she ever been found? No, a quick Google search revealed that Maren Wolf was still among the missing, almost two decades later. Over the years, there'd been many attempts to find her, and her face had been placed on the back of many milk cartons, but eventually, the trail had gone cold. Maren Wolf had all but vanished, and her little sister was the sole survivor of the tragedy.

Ah, so that explained Rylie Wolf's sadness. And her profession—had she gone into the FBI with hopes of avenging these crimes against her family?

I knew we had something in common, little Wolf. You can't forget about your family, either.

He found a recent photograph of her and stared at her face until it was burned into his memory. She was a discriminating woman. A beautiful piece of art, herself, with that long cinnamon hair and that freckled skin. Her flaws made her infinitely more interesting than the typical magazine cover model. She was the stuff of legend, something impossible to ever replicate.

Someone like her couldn't simply be taken. She had to be won.

In order to do that, he needed to impress her, first.

And he knew just how to do it.

CHAPTER TWENTY FOUR

Letter in hand, Rylie left the rest of the conference room and wandered out toward the lobby. "Excuse me," she said to the older officer there. "Were you on duty when this letter came in?"

She nodded sheepishly. "I'm so sorry. I must've been busy with my files. I don't remember seeing the guy at all."

Rylie nodded. As she stood there, staring out the doors, it occurred to her.

The killer had been right here.

He'd opened these doors. He'd tread along these floor tiles. He'd leaned up against this counter and had words with one of the officers. He'd been so close.

And yet, she still had no idea what to do in order to catch him.

Her breathing quickened, her chest started to close up, and she knew what was coming. Growing up, after the tragedy, she'd had these panic attacks often.

Swallowing, she went for the door.

"Hey, where are you going?" Brisbane called behind her, but she waved him away and rushed outside, still gripping the photocopy of the letter in her hands.

She'd hoped the fresh air would help her catch her breath, but it didn't work. Her vision started to swim.

She picked up her phone and called the only person who understood. "Hello?"

"Hal?"

"Is that you, Rylie, baby girl? Long time no hear. What's going on?"

Immediately, her breathing returned to normal. Hal Buxton was like magic that way. He owned the ranch bordering hers, and though he lived on a trailer in the middle of it, all by himself, he had more land. Rylie's father and Hal had a bit of a rivalry, for a time. Mr. Wolf had called Hal a crazy old loon and forbid Rylie and Maren from ever playing near his land. Their father had made the man into a monster.

But shortly after the death of her mother and disappearance of Maren, Rick Wolf had turned in on himself, drinking a lot, barely getting out of bed most days. In her grief, Rylie had run away. She found herself, miles away from home and hungry, when a storm hit, and she had taken refuge in an old barn.

Hal's old barn.

He'd taken her in, fed her, and talked to her. Turned out, he was a lonely man whose wife had died five years prior. He was a good man, and they'd become friends. He understood when she had her panic attacks, and knew just what to do to keep the demons at bay.

"Hi, Hal."

"What's wrong, girl? Life all right in Seattle?"

His gentle voice made her smile. "I'm actually here in Wyoming."

"Wyoming? And you didn't think to come say hi to me?"

She laughed. "It's funny, but Wyoming's not all that close to your place."

"Eh. It's closer than Seattle. What're you doing down there? Working on a new case?"

"Yeah, actually." He'd always loved hearing about her many interesting cases. Nothing much happened there in Montana, so he relied on her to give him some news. "It's what looks like a serial killer."

"No kidding! You better stay safe, girl."

"I'm safe," she said, though looking down at the letter, she wasn't sure how true that was. "But I'm running into dead ends and I have to admit, it's getting me down."

"Yeah? Well, I'm sure you'll figure it out."

That was Hal. He had the ultimate faith in her and her abilities, even when her father had failed her. "I don't know about this one. They all seem so random. And if I can't come up with a connection, I'm afraid I'll never be able to pinpoint where he'll strike next."

"How many has he killed?"

"So far, four that we know of. The bodies were found at mile markers along eighty-six."

"The Devil's Highway?" He whistled, "Well, that makes sense. He killed hitchhikers, huh?"

"No, he . . ."

Suddenly, something struck her. She'd been so busy concentrating on the place where these people had been left. But really, she had more information than that. She hadn't given Beeker the coordinates for where they'd been taken from. If she gave Beeker that information, maybe another pattern would emerge.

"Baby girl? You all right?" Hal said.

"Oh, yes. Forget it," she said finally. "I just had an idea."

"I knew you would. What?"

"Well, I was always thinking about how he left all the victims at a mile marker, so that was likely significant. But I never thought about it in relation to where the victim was taken from." Her mind whirled with possibilities. "I just hope we can do something to stop him before he strikes again."

"Yeah. Well . . . if the mile markers are so important to him, why don't you get rid of them?"

She nearly laughed aloud. Hal always had a strange, out-of-the-box way of thinking. "Yeah, great idea, Hal," she said, smiling. He always made her feel better. "I'll call and catch up again later. Now I have to get back to work."

"Okay, Baby. Take care of yourself."

She ended the call and rushed back inside. She sat down next to Beeker, who was typing like a madman, and waited for him to stop. When he didn't, she said, "Beeker?"

"Huh?"

"I have an idea."

He stopped and looked at her.

She was about to launch into her plan when she realized he had a line of chocolate on his upper lip, mingling with the fine, reddish stubble. "Do you have a chocolate moustache?"

Embarrassed, he wiped his mouth with the back of his hand. "Uh. Sorry. I had hot chocolate. What's your idea?"

She pointed to the computer. "I realized we only gave you the locations of the mileposts where the bodies were found. But what if you enter in the locations where the people were abducted from? Would that produce a clearer idea?"

Brisbane came up behind her and sat down to have a front-row view. "Right . . ."

Beeker nodded. "It could, but do you have that information?"

"Not for all the murders. But for the others, we have a pretty good estimation."

"All right. Well, give it to me. I'll see what we've got."

She rattled off the different exits and locations where the victims had last been seen. Darla McCrea, at the St. Xavier exit. Tonya Birch, at the Happy Donut Café at the exit for Fort Winston. Cody Thompson, somewhere on the highway between Sheridan and headquarters. The cases of Preston Baker and Nancy Sharpe, she pulled out the information from their police report as to where they had last been seen. At least, now, they had something to go on.

Beeker entered the coordinates into his program and they waited for the computer to produce the results. Rylie stared at the screen, not wanting to blink for fear of missing something. When the screen blinked, it said, *One result found.*

"What does that mean? There's only one place he can strike next?" Rylie asked.

He nodded. "Yeah. It's saying with eighty-six percent probability that the next murder will happen at seventy-three."

"How can it say that?" Rylie said, staring at it in wonder. "What makes it so sure this time? Because—"

"Because you look at the numbers. 61, 67, 83, 97, 101. The other ones—71 and 79 are actual exits. So they don't have mileposts."

Brisbane squinted. "I don't get it. The other what? What are you talking about? There are dozens of other mileposts in between there that it can be."

"Yeah, but seventy-three is the only one."

"The only what?" Rylie asked, exasperated.

"Prime number."

Brisbane frowned. "Prime . . ."

Beeker let out a superior sigh. "It's a number that can only be divided by one and its—"

"I know," Brisbane waved him away, staring at the screen. Then he looked at Rylie. "It's probably the best chance we've had this whole time."

"Probably? Try *definitely*," she said, heading for the door. "Are you going to drive like a little sissy, or should I drive?"

He snorted. "Wait. Let's take our time here."

She stopped and frowned at him, tapping her toe. "Why?"

"Because what difference does it make if we stake out 73? That's not where he finds his victims—it's where he leaves them. And if we want to stop him from killing again, we've got to be smart about this."

She stopped tapping her toe and let out a sigh. He was right. The best outcome would be if they could stop him from killing again. But what could they do, especially when they had no idea where he'd find this next victim?

A crazy thought settled into her brain, one that she hadn't considered before, because it was so laughable. Now, it seemed to make perfect sense.

She slammed both palms on the table.

"I think I have an idea," she announced.

CHAPTER TWENTY FIVE

"Are you insane?"

Rylie paced the floor of the conference room, clenching and unclenching her fists. She hadn't been sure about very much in this case, but when the idea popped into her mind, she knew, as crazy as it'd sounded, it was the right one.

"I'm not insane. It makes total sense," she said, fixing them each, in turn, with a level stare. "Think about it."

"I am thinking about it," Sparks said, running his hands through his thinning hair. "And I think it's ludicrous. You want us to remove how many mileposts, from where to where?"

She nodded. "Yes. From about 61 to 103. I think that should be good."

"Why?"

"Because if that's where he's going to dump the body, we need to confuse him." She looked at Brisbane. "Remember Cody Thompson? He was still warm when we came across the body. That means that the killer likely abducts them somewhere and then kills them in the car, on the side of the road, before he sets them out on the milepost. He kills them at the scene, but in his car. So if we remove the milepost, he won't be able to find the right place. You see?"

Brisbane stared at her, and for a moment, she could see the doubt in his face. He didn't believe in her. Wouldn't help her.

Damn.

This was exactly why she didn't want and had never wanted a partner.

She threw up her hands. "Fine. If you don't believe me, we'll do it your way. Send police to the exits around seventy-three tonight, hoping someone will see him." She shook her head. "But I still say that's too risky. It's only two. We still have time to remove the mileposts."

The men all stared at each other, daring one another to be the first to speak.

"Come on. Bris," she said, giving him a pleading look.

He broke their gaze and looked at the table, shaking his head slightly, and for a moment she was sure he was going to tell her to forget about it. But then he said, “All right. Sparks, let’s do this. Is there a road crew we can send out to get it done?”

Rylie stared at him in shock and relief.

Sparks’s gaze shifted between the two of them. Finally, he said, “Yeah. I guess I can make some phone calls. If worse comes to worst, I’ll send my men out.”

As he left, Rylie smiled at her partner. “Thank you, Agent. I didn’t expect you to give in.”

“Don’t get used to it,” he grumbled. “I still think it’s a stupid idea.”

But as he walked away, she thought she detected a hint of a smile.

*

Daylight was waning, and the bitter Wyoming wind was beginning to pick up as their truck pulled up to what would’ve been milepost 73, if it had been marked. Thankfully, though, a team of road workers had swept through, a bit earlier, and removed all of the markings. The only thing left was a deep hole in the grass where the post had once been buried. They’d had to carefully count the miles from the previous exit in order to find it.

I hope this works, Rylie thought, staring out the window at the brown, rolling hills.

“Looks like everything’s set,” Brisbane said, stretching. “So what do you want to do in the meantime? Late lunch? Early dinner?”

She shook her head. How he could think about food at a time like this was beyond her. She said, “I think we should go to the exits before and after this one, and check them out. There’s a good chance the next victim will be picked up at one of those, don’t you think?”

“Yeah. I guess. Exits 71 and 79, huh?” He started up the car and navigated out onto the road. “But we should get something to eat if we’re going to be staking out this place by nightfall.”

“Sure,” she said, rolling her eyes. “Your treat.”

He shrugged. “Fried chicken. I really want KFC.”

“Whatever,” she said, as they made their way to the nearest exit, 71. The exit was for a state historic park with a museum of Native American artifacts. As they exited, that was the first thing they saw—a small log cabin with a large parking area, across the street from a small gas station.

"This place is pretty busy," he said, pulling into the lot.

Actually, it was. The lot was huge, but there were ten or twelve cars parked there, more than what Rylie would've expected, considering the place was very much in the middle of nowhere. When he pulled into a parking spot and she stepped out, looking around, all she could see, for miles, were hills, stretching out into the distance, toward the Bighorn Mountains.

Brisbane strode over to a sign in front of the building. "This is the former site of a Crow settlement."

She scanned the area. "Okay. But can we focus on what we're looking for?"

His lips twisted as he shielded his eyes from the sun with his hand. "Okay. What are we looking for, again?"

She swept her eyes over the cars. A couple of sportscars. A Jeep. An SUV. No light-colored sedan. She sighed. "I don't know. Anything suspicious."

As they stood there, in front of the stout building, a young, striking woman with long blonde hair came out of the front double doors. She was wearing Uggs and a big flannel shirt with tight, ripped blue jeans, and playing with her cell phone. She almost didn't see Rylie until she'd nearly walked straight into her.

Alarms went off in Rylie's head. *Now, there's someone the killer would target.*

But that wasn't necessarily true. The killer had targeted all kinds of people—men, women, old, young. The only common factor among all the victims was that they'd been alone.

And as oblivious as she was, she was a good target. Rylie watched her, scraping her teeth over her lower lip, wondering if she should say something.

Brisbane was watching, too, clearly concerned. He nudged Rylie and was about to speak, when the door opened and a tall, lanky kid stepped out, running to catch up with the girl. He squeezed her to his side and the two walked off to their Jeep Wrangler, completely unaware of the FBI agents' scrutiny.

"Forget it," Brisbane said, rubbing his hands together. He pointed to the museum. "Want to check inside?"

They went in and walked around in a circle. The place smelled heavily of incense and sage, and the whole museum was a single room. There were a few families, navigating through the artifacts and exhibits. Two male museum workers. An older couple. No young, scruffy man in a hoodie. Nobody who even looked anything like the man they'd seen in the video.

When they were back outside, Rylie said, "What about if we go and check out exit 79?"

"Good idea." Brisbane fished in his pockets for his keys. "But let's go to the gas station across the street, first. I've got to fill up."

He navigated to the Gas Extravaganza across the street and went to fill up. As he stepped out of the car to fill his tank, she yawned.

She didn't need Kentucky Fried Chicken. She needed a bigger pick-me-up if they were going to spend the upcoming night, staking out the milepost.

She got out. "I'm going to get a coffee. Want one?"

He nodded. "Fine. But promise me we'll get that chicken?"

"Yeah, yeah, yeah," she mumbled, waving him away as she went to the convenience store.

It was a small place, packed with the barest of necessities, though it did have an impressive array of donuts in glass shelves, behind the counter. The coffee service was pretty good, too. She poured two of the largest commuter cups, fastened on the lids, and went to the register to pay.

But there was no one there. "Hello?" she called, peering into what looked like a small break room attached to the back of the store.

Nothing.

There were a few coins scattered on the counter. Maybe, in this part of the world, they still believed people were generally good and honest and went by the honor system. She didn't usually carry cash, but luckily, she happened to have a five-dollar-bill in her wallet. She pulled it out and slapped it on the counter.

"Thank you!" she called, just in case someone was nearby, then took one cup in each hand and turned to leave.

She only made it two steps when she noticed something on the ground.

It was small, barely the size of a dime. Steadying the coffee in her hands, she stooped to look at it.

Brick red, and still wet. Fresh.

Blood.

Straightening, she looked around.

That was when she saw another one. A few steps closer to the door, a dark red splotch of blood.

She pushed open the door with her body and walked through the lot, keeping her eyes trained on the ground, looking for the next breadcrumb on the trail. It wasn't much blood, so she didn't know what to make of it. If she'd seen it anywhere else, she'd have assumed one of the customers had a small cut, or a bloody nose.

But knowing what she knew, about a killer being in the midst, her heart thumped as she stepped between the cars parked in front of the store.

"What are you doing?" Brisbane called to her from the pumps.

Rylie ignored him, scanning around for another drop. Seeing nothing, she raised her eyes to one of the cars, and noticed something that made her freeze in her tracks.

Brisbane called over to her again from his truck. "What's going on?"

"I don't—"

Her words died in her throat and her blood turned to ice.

Right underneath the door handle, there were several drops of congealed blood, dripping a lazy, zig-zagging pattern down to the asphalt below.

CHAPTER TWENTY SIX

The woman in the back seat of his sedan let out a low moan.

"There, there," he said, checking over his shoulder. "You'll be all right."

It wasn't a lie. She'd be much better, once she realized what a grand and glorious thing she'd be a part of. In her ordinary life, she'd been nothing special. A clerk at a convenience store attached to the gas station. She'd probably made minimum wage there, scraping by, every day, wondering if it would ever be possible to make her mark on the world. Maybe she'd already given up on the day-to-day drudgery of her life, accepting that she'd never be anything important. Just like her parents probably told her, every day of her life.

Now, she would prove them all wrong.

She moaned again.

"No, no. You don't have to thank me," he said lightly, smiling into the mirror at her. "The look on your face will be thanks enough."

He frowned as he noticed something. There was a long line of blood trickling down her cheek, from when he'd hit her in the head.

Dammit. That wasn't supposed to be there.

He banged the heel of his hand on his forehead, hard, in frustration. The blood wasn't part of his vision. He'd imagine a clean face on this masterpiece.

But he'd had no choice. When he'd loosened the rock from the pathway at the Gas Extravaganza near the highway exit, he'd expected to sneak up on her from behind as she stocked the shelves behind the counter with donuts. He'd watched her, and she'd been standing with her back to the register for twenty good minutes, just arranging things as people went in and out of the store, leaving their change for their coffees on the counter. So when he stepped inside, he thought she'd continue on, doing the same.

But then she'd turned, and the rock had caught her on the side of the head, instead of the back.

Everything else had been pure poetry, just as he'd planned. She'd collapsed like a house of cards behind the cash register, a couple of jelly donuts still clutched in her plastic-gloved hands. He'd easily lifted her onto his shoulder and carried her out to his car, placing her in the backseat. Despite it being broad daylight, no one was the wiser.

That place made shitty donuts, like bricks. Always had. And their gas had always been too expensive. Still, it was busy, because it was the only place for miles. But the people there were too busy going from place to place to pay attention. People didn't pay attention anymore.

It had been all too easy, all too problem-free.

Until now.

The blood would be a problem. He'd have to clean her up before he finished his work.

Oh well, he thought, imagining what his father would say. *Into every day, a little rain must fall.* That's what his momma had said, anyway, when she'd told him he couldn't go to art school in Philadelphia.

She'd done her thing. She'd gone to Harvard, become a great mathematician. Why she'd come to this corner of hell and fallen in love with a rancher was beyond anyone's guess. And why she didn't see, why she didn't try to help him realize his dream was another thing, entirely. She was too meek. In the end, she'd given up everything, even teaching her classes at the local college, to play wifey to that asshole.

She'd never stuck up for him. Not once. Years of working, of slaving, just to get away from this one-horse shithole, only to get that acceptance to the finest art school in the country, and his father had tossed it away like it was nothing. He was always doing that, belittling his art, calling it sissy shit. *Learn to work with your hands, boy. Man the ranch. That's the real work. Real men work the land. Our ancestors always had.*

But he didn't want to. No matter how many times he'd told his parents he was meant for something else, something greater, it never sunk in. Usually, he earned a fist in the face for it—and that was when he was lucky. Sometimes, when his father was drunk, he'd use a shovel, or a branding iron. Sometimes, it'd even be hot, and he still had the scars to show for it.

Despite all the hardship, though, he'd managed to find greatness. Right here, in Wyoming, he'd made a mark. He'd achieved a new kind of artistry that the world had never seen. It'd started with small animals, and progressed to larger ones. There was never a shortage of those, and his father was usually too drunk to keep count. Year after year, he honed his craft, until he decided it was time to move on to bigger and better things.

Things like this beautiful specimen, here.

Damn that blood. It would make things more difficult. How would she be his masterpiece, with that?

He stared at his gnarled knuckles on the wheel. They weren't the gentle hands of an artist anymore. They were of someone he wasn't supposed to be. A man who'd had his purpose in life beaten out of him.

He was shaken from those thoughts by another low moan. He wiped an eye, surprised to find he had tears in them, and looked up to see the woman stirring.

Shit. He thought he'd gotten her better than that.

No matter, he thought, as he pulled onto the highway. He'd finish her soon.

"What am I doing here?" the woman suddenly screeched, looking around, frantic.

Oh, great. A hysteric. Just what he needed. "Calm yourself. You had an accident. I'm taking you to the hospital."

Her head lolled, and it appeared she was having trouble keeping her eyes open. Her voice was sleepy. "What? No . . . where am I?"

"Just calm down. Go to sleep. We'll be there soon."

That didn't satisfy her. "Please. Please don't hurt me."

"I'm not hurting you. I'm helping you," he bit off each word in frustration. "Now if you'll just shut your—"

"Please! Don't hurt my baby! I'm pregnant!"

Fuck. She wasn't going to believe him, no matter what he said, so he decided not to continue on with the charade. It was pissing him off, anyway. "You're a lying little bitch, aren't you?"

"No, it's true! I swear!"

She was coming to, now, getting more lucid. He didn't have the time. He stepped on the gas, looking for the next milepost so he could see how much farther he had to go. "Shut up. Not a word out of you."

She began to sob quietly. "Please . . . please . . .."

Groaning, he turned up the music on his radio. It was Mahler, his favorite. He always loved to create to Mahler. He took a deep breath, trying to let the music invade his senses, take over, calm him, all the while watching the side of the road.

Wait a minute.

He'd grown up here. Traveled these roads all the time. He remembered that burned out shack on the side of the road, now just a pile of rubble and rotted wood with overgrown weeds. There should've been a mile marker in front of it.

But there wasn't one.

Some drunk fool probably knocked it down with their pickup. Stupid hicks around here, just like my daddy.

He drove on, looking for the next one. He drove and drove, but it wasn't there, either. Instead, he came across the next exit.

Stiffening, he wondered, for the first time, what in hell's name was going on.

Then it hit him.

Rylie Wolf.

The FBI agent. The smart one.

She'd done this. Crazy, beautiful spitfire had removed the goddamn mileposts.

Well played, Wolf.

He hadn't stopped thinking about her, since he Googled her and learned all about her hard life. Little Miss Convenience Store had been for her. When he'd imagined what this next work of art would look like, he'd imagined Rylie Wolf's face as she saw it. Appreciated it. The whole composition was to please her.

So why was she doing this to him?

He shook his head and navigated to the next exit, preparing to turn around.

She simply didn't understand. Not yet. But she would.

He'd make sure of it.

CHAPTER TWENTY SEVEN

The FBI agents raced down the highway, headed for 73, the milepost where Rylie was sure she'd find the next victim.

"Broad daylight," Brisbane kept saying, again and again. "He's getting bolder. He had to have kidnapped her in broad daylight."

"I think she worked at that shop," Rylie said, her pulse pounding. "There was no one in there. And then I saw drops of blood. I think he kidnapped her from there."

"Why was there blood on that car door?"

"Think about it." She *had* been thinking about it. It was all she'd been doing. "He comes up to her while she's behind the counter. Hits her on the head and knocks her out. She's bleeding. He lifts her onto his shoulder and carries her out to his car, so that her head is behind him. Maybe he pauses to open the door, to get things ready for her. The blood would drip onto the door of the car next to him, her car."

Brisbane nodded. "Shit. You think she's still alive?"

"I hope she is." She stared at the mile markers on her phone. With the mileposts gone, their GPS was the only way to find the right place. "Three more miles."

"I can't believe he'd do this in broad daylight. Why would he take the chance?"

Rylie shrugged. "He's been doing it all along. Switching things up, trying to make it harder to be caught. Yes, it's a risk for him to take someone in daylight, but at least he knows we won't be looking for him, then."

"Yeah."

For once, Brisbane was driving above the speed limit, pushing ninety. She was so busy staring at her GPS that she almost didn't see the gray sedan on the side of the road until they'd gone past it.

"Stop!" she said.

He slammed ungracefully on the brakes and winced as the tires squealed under him and his car fishtailed, emitting the smell of burned rubber. He glanced in his rearview mirror as he navigated to the side of the road. "Was that what I thought it was?"

"A light-colored sedan?" She studied it in the side mirror as the dust around them settled. Then she pushed open the door and looked back at it. "Yep. Sure looks like one, to me."

"Shit." He tried to look back himself. "Can you see anyone?"

"No. The driver's side looks empty. But the passenger side door is open."

He reached for the gun in his shoulder holster. "Let's think this through. Here's what we should do. We'll call in--"

"No time," she said, reaching for her own gun and jumping out. "Come on."

Letting out a curse, he followed her. By the time he met her at the tailgate, he'd taken his gun from his holster, too. Together, in slow, deliberate movements, they raised their guns and proceeded toward the sedan, one on either side of it.

"This is the FBI," Rylie shouted. "Come out with your hands up."

Nothing.

She took another step forward, and Brisbane followed her lead, until the two of them were even with the front bumper of the car. From there, she could see it for certain—there was no one in the car. "He's gone. Shit."

Brisbane leaned over and put his hand on the hood. "Still warm. He was just here. Did we miss him?"

"I don't know." She'd just begun to lower her gun and look around when she heard it.

Muffled, terrified cries.

"Do you hear that?" Brisbane said.

She nodded and made her way to the open door. When she looked inside, she saw a woman, in the back seat, bleeding and bound. She brought her fingers to her throat to check her pulse. She was alive. He'd meant for her to be his next victim, but they'd stopped him.

A surge of relief and pride coursed through her, but it was short-lived. He was still out there.

"Shit," Brisbane said again, scanning the area. "Where do you think he went?"

Rylie's eyes shifted across the barren landscape. It stretched out as far as the eye could see, bleak, brown hills, with only an odd tree or two in sight. There were mountains, studded with impressive log cabins, too far in the distance. If the killer had been in this car, only moments ago, he'd be in sight, unless he was a master of disguise, a chameleon who could melt into the landscape.

She was just about to answer that she had no idea when she saw it. A flash of a black shirt and white skin, in the distance.

"There!"

Brisbane saw it a second later, when she'd already begun to scurry down the embankment toward her target, gun at the ready. "Wait, where do you think—"

She reached level ground and started to tear across the plateau, after him. "Just stay with the victim and call in the cops!" she called over her shoulder.

He was screaming something after her, but she couldn't hear. The strong Wyoming wind roared in her ears as she pumped her legs and arms, dashing over the uneven, scrub-brush covered dirt. She threw herself through a line of bushes, jumping over a small ravine, and rocketed toward him, to the point where she was running so hard, she hardly felt the ground beneath her feet.

Her vision bounced as she swept her gaze over the horizon, her gaze zeroing in on the man in the black sweatshirt. He was closer now, loping at a fairly casual pace. She could see his face—his doughy cheeks, covered in blonde stubble, his black baseball cap, his …

It set off alarms in her head. Did he know he was being pursued? Did he care? Did he want to be caught now?

Or was this some kind of trap?

She couldn't think about it, wouldn't allow herself to think about anything else but pinning her quarry. She needed this man caught, off the streets, forever. Nothing else mattered.

With that thought firm in her mind, she surged forward, leaping over a bush.

It was only when she hit the ground that she realized she'd lost sight of him. There was an old shack in the distance, part of what was likely an old mining community. She skidded to a stop on the loose gravel, looking around. The adrenaline pulsing through her veins seemed to freeze, and the first tendrils of fear snaked up her back.

Where was he?

Clenching her gun in her fist, she scanned the area, noting all the places that he could hide. There were only three that she could see. One was a low bush. Another, a pile of rocks. Another, the remains of the destroyed shed.

Something moved behind the shed, a shadow. It was a split-second movement, hardly noticeable at all, but in an instant, it took all her concentration.

Raising her gun, she moved toward it.

"This is the FBI," she said, keeping her voice even. "I need you to come out with your hands up."

She didn't expect him to give in that easy. He didn't. Keeping her eyes trained on the edge of the shed, she crept closer, her finger grazing the trigger, ready to pull.

When she finally reached the corner of the shed, she shifted slightly to see around it.

There was nothing but a couple of weeds, swaying in the wind.

Her heart leapt into her throat as she heard the crunching of earth beneath her.

This isn't good, was the only thing she thought, along with a fleeting memory of her instructors at the Academy. *You never want to get to the point of hand-to-hand combat with an assailant. Especially you, Princess.*

Before she could turn, he was on her, something raised over his head. It came down on her, grazing the side of her cheek, and the pain was immediate, exquisite. She let out a cry and tried to level her gun at him, but he swept another arm at her from out of nowhere, knocking her in the elbow. The force was too much. She felt the gun slip from her fingers, heard it thud on the ground behind her.

But he kept coming. Unstoppable. Unwavering. He was at least a foot taller than her, and though slim, his body was full of muscle.

His face was white as dough, and he had blonde stubble of a kid who tried and failed to grow a beard. In fact, his face was so boyish, Rylie had a hard time thinking he was more than fifteen or sixteen years old. His eyes were wide as a baby's, blue as the sky, and yet, filled with the malice and hate of someone far older, far more jaded.

He reached for her throat, attempting to lock his hands around her. She swept her arms out, flailing them, as she'd learned in Academy. Staggering backwards, she tried to sight her gun on the ground.

No good. She thought it'd landed in the weeds, but it wasn't there.

Frantic, she faced her assailant once again. He came charging for her, lips twisted in rage. She leapt to the side, and his head made contact with her ribs. Something inside her cracked and shifted as he lodged her up against the back of the broken shed.

"Why are you doing this?" she asked as he took a place on top of her again, lifting and spinning her around to try and get at her neck. As he spun her, she shot out her right hand, fingers pencil-straight, and slammed fingertips into the base of his neck, just above his collarbone.

He gasped and took a step back, surprised by the sudden offense. As he faltered, she dragged herself back upright and struck again, this time with the edge of her hand, drove it into his shoulder right at a nerve cluster. Another Academy move. He grunted and stumbled again, his fingers flexing. “Bitch.”

He raised his head and glared at her with a face from the depths of Hell itself. Eyes wide and crazed, tiny circular pupils swimming in a raging ocean of white, streaked with red. Nostrils flared, teeth gnashing, and his face a shade of violent crimson. Throughout his throat, raised veins bulged into thickened muscle tissue.

She took a step back, trying to regain some sense of balance, forgetting the shed behind her. Its rough, splintered surface caught on the fabric of her shirt and hair, pulling strands of it sharply as she sprang forward. He leapt at her, screaming, a bellow of unadulterated hatred. She tried to sidestep him again, skirting out of the way, but he crashed into her hip, and they both went hurtling against the wood of the shed, which gave way with an enormous crack.

The splintering wood opened up and dumped them both over and onto the dirt floor of the shed, in a tangle of flesh and thrashing arms. One of his fists collided with her jaw as he tried to gain some kind of advantage in the twisted embrace, but Rylie thrust out her elbow a second later, striking him in the shoulder, knocking him away. Clambering to her feet, she backpedaled, trying to get some space, but he was already up on his feet and moving towards her. She stumbled over something on the ground in effort to get away, and he locked his hands on her shoulders again, slamming her up against another broken wall of the shed.

"Why?" she asked again. "Just tell me why—"

He wasn’t buying it this time. He was a man possessed. No amount of distraction would work.

"No more talk. I'm going to fucking kill you, Wolf."

Wolf. He knew her name.

"I don't understand." Her throat was in agony, a scratchy, arid desert, so she could only whisper the words. He moved one of his hands back to her neck, pressing her against the wall and cutting off her airway.

"You don’t? Of all people, I thought you would. I expected better of you," he growled so that she could barely hear him. Her eyes and ears filled with water, and she felt like she was drowning. He pushed again, and black swarmed her vision. "I expected you would appreciate this."

Her left hand dropped as her vision shifted from black to white, and she struggled for breath. Half-formed thoughts assaulted her brain, little scraps of memory, of her mother, of Maren, dancing outside the RV. The only thing she could feel was the press of his flesh against her neck and the massive weight against her shoulder as he held her against the wall.

Soon, she'd be dead. Like her mother. Her death wouldn't affect anyone's as much as her mother's had affected Rylie's and her father's, but it would do one thing.

It would allow this asshole the freedom to kill again.

And maybe, likely, the next time he killed, it would be someone who was everything to another person. And it would destroy that person's life, just as hers had been, all those years ago.

With that thought, her eyes flew open. She forced herself to focus, to regroup. Her limbs were going numb at her side, but they were still useful. Instead of flailing helplessly, she concentrated on finding her pocket. Fingers delving into the fabric of her jacket, they closed around her car keys, the jagged ends poking out from between the knuckles of her clenched fist. Ripping her hand from her pocket, she put every ounce of life she had left into a single strike.

Up. As fast and as hard as she could.

It caught him off-guard. The mixture of flesh, bone, and metal slammed him just underneath the chin, and he made a strange gurgle and choke, releasing her throat.

She dropped to her knees, gasping for precious air, as he stumbled backwards, screaming with a loud and uncontrolled volume, a bellow more than a shout. He tripped over the same rock that Rylie had stumbled upon, but scrambled to his feet, a hand still clutched to the bottom half of his face.

"God damn you!" he shouted. "Damn you!"

She couldn't think of a single witty retort as she knelt there, her throat raw and barely pulling in oxygen. Her back and shoulders were one cascading wave of torn agony, and when he took a step toward her, all she could think was, *No more*.

Everything she'd done, fighting him off, wasn't enough. She'd wanted to get the better of him, she'd wanted it desperately, but he was too strong for her. Too great. He stood and staggered toward her, fists clenched, his face drowned in dim shadow.

Still gasping, every muscle in her body protesting, she could do nothing but watch him come. She could still feel the keys wedged in her fist, and clenched it tighter, bringing one leg up into a half-kneel, ready to launch another attack, but the starbursts flared behind her eyes with every motion. .

He took another step, easing around the stumbling rock, and reached for her, pulling her up by the collar of her shirt. She smelled his rancid breath and opened her eyes to find him glaring at her with nothing but hate. He snarled then lifted her up, into his arms, tossing her up over his broad shoulder so that the world went end over end.

"What?" she began, but she wasn't sure if she was thinking it or actually saying it. Her heart was beating too hard for her to hear anything but its rapid rhythm.

He was taking her somewhere. She bobbed against his broad back with every footstep. It occurred to her to clench her fists and pummel his back, but she couldn't summon the energy.

Then, suddenly, she was hurled forward, and she felt herself falling, down, down, down, weightless. She didn't have time to tense or brace herself before her head hit the ground, and then her legs, in a heap. The pain was like nothing she'd ever felt before, shooting down her spine from the base of her skull. Her body settled into something cold and powdery, and a sharp intake of breath gave her nothing but musty, chalky air that coated her lungs.

Where am I? With effort, she opened her eyes and saw nothing but black.

Night.

Her skull screamed as she tilted her head up and saw a light.

Daylight. So it was still day.

But the light was very, very far away. The black was warm and calm and comforting, and she wanted to go there, more than anything. So she let the black come. She let the black take her away.

CHAPTER TWENTY EIGHT

Run. Hide.

That was what Rose had said to her, before she'd gone outside the RV. She'd smiled at her, in that warm way she always had while watching the girls, but there was something in her eyes that had given Rylie pause.

Fear.

She'd hidden, deep in the back bedroom, farthest from the door. Covered herself with blankets and prayed, even as she heard the door to the RV swinging open, and strange male voices, filling the space. *"I thought there were three?"* one had said.

"Naw. Just those two."

And then the door had slammed, and after that, nothing.

Nothing for hours and hours. Or at least, it seemed like that. Rylie had been bathed in sweat by the time she'd pulled herself out from her hiding spot. She'd crept to the dirt-crusted window over the RV's kitchenette sink and stared out at the bodies, lying motionless in a circle.

And then . . .

Rylie woke with a start, and immediately she felt the ache.

It was everywhere, all-encompassing, from her toes to the top of her head. She'd been contorted into such an odd position, while she'd been in that RV, hiding, but she'd never felt a pain such as this.

She tried to move, to flex the muscles of her back, but the pain was even worse, screaming up her spine. Tearing open a single eyelid, she followed the shaft of dim light upward, over a narrow, rocky wall. She could only tilt her head back so far—the pain was too much—but it was enough to see an opening, up above.

Suddenly, it came to her. The fight with that man. The rundown shack in the middle of the barren land.

A mine. She'd fallen in a mine shaft.

She choked on the dust, which coated her throat, chalky and acrid. Her eyes adjusted to the scenery around her. She was at the bottom of the shaft, but ahead of her, it appeared to go on, for only a short distance, before ending in a heap of rubble and darkness.

Her spine was twisted unnaturally. She tried to straighten it and managed to do so, just as a giant spider skittered down her arm.

Shaking it off, she looked around for something, some kind of ladder or series of footholds that she could use to help herself up. It was then that she realized her legs and wrists were bound by a thin coil of rope. She shook her hands, her legs, but the ties were too tight.

She was trapped.

"Help," she said, but it came out too softly. She had no saliva left in her mouth at all.

A trickle of sweat found its way over the bridge of her nose, seeping down into her eyes. Blinking so she wouldn't lose focus, she tried to think.

That was when a shape appeared from the darkness behind her. "You couldn't leave well enough alone, could you, Agent?" the voice said, leaning over her. It wasn't as gravelly as she'd expected—instead, it was rather feminine, but his body was anything but. His form was large and imposing, silhouetted by the light above.

The killer.

"What do you have to say for yourself?"

Before she could think to try to scream, there was the sound of ripping duct tape, and then the seal was pressed over her dry lips, effectively trapping all sound within her throat. The most she could let out was a gurgling snort.

She would die down here, alone, silent. Terror threatened to grip her, but she held it back, swinging her head around, trying to find some escape.

Brisbane. He wasn't far behind her. He'd come looking for her, eventually. Wouldn't he?

She wasn't entirely sure. She couldn't remember the last time she'd seen him. It had been at the killer's car, hadn't it? His victim had been in the back seat, tied up. Hadn't that happened? Or was that all a dream? Her head swam. The fall down here—she had fallen here, hadn't she?— had done a number on her. She couldn't remember, couldn't separate fact from the fantasy in her head.

Pulling her eyes open, she watched as the man straightened. A ray of light shone down upon his face, fully illuminating it for the first time. His blue eyes blazed with determination, with insanity. "Now, you're going to die down here," he said with a smile of satisfaction. "But don't worry. You won't stay down here. I won't let that happen."

She swallowed and tasted blood.

"No. I need someone to be on mile marker seventy-three," he said with a laugh. "It was going to be that girl. But it might as well be you. It doesn't really matter."

"Why . . .," she started, forgetting her mouth was covered. It came out as a *Mmmm.*

But as crazy as the man in front of her was, he was intuitive, intelligent, too. He understood. "Why do I care about mile markers, you ask? Well, that's simple." There was a broken crate in the discarded rubble. He picked it up, settled it down next to her, and lowered his big body onto it, as if preparing to tell her a fairy tale. "My asshole father."

She wanted to ask questions. Anything to prolong this, to make him take his time. But he didn't need questions. He crossed one leg over the other, as if he intended to stretch this tale out over a long period of time.

"Yes, I know what you're thinking," he said with a small, mischievous smile. "Oh, just another killer who was traumatized as a child. That's what the stupid person might see. But anyone who really looked into it would see so much more. You, Rylie, can see that, yes? I know you've experienced trauma as well, yes?"

Her eyes widened. Did he know? So as long as she'd been looking into him, he'd been looking into her as well? She shivered.

"Ah, yes. I do know all about your family. And I do know your name, Rylie Wolf. I suppose I should tell you who I am, since we haven't been properly introduced." He leaned over and grasped her bound hand, shaking it slightly. "I'm Fergus. Fergus McAdams."

Fergus McAdams. The name didn't ring a bell at all. After all the suspects and names that had been compiled in the files, that one had been completely ignored. Even with all those murders, he'd flown totally under the radar, all this time.

"It is a shame. I do like you, Agent. I feel like in another time or another place, we could be fast friends. Maybe even lovers."

She cringed.

"Oh, I know, I'm not much to look at. But I have other qualities that no doubt, you'd find attractive. See, we both experienced trauma. And I suppose trauma has a way of making a person go one of two ways. Either they decide to fight crime, to stop it from happening to anyone else. Like you. Or they're more like me. More practical. They realize that bad things are going to happen, so they might as well play a part in it. Make it interesting. Give ordinary people meaning in their lives. Me? I like to bring beauty to the world. Yes, I suppose people like you might see it as crime, but is it? Is it, when it elevates an ordinary subject, making them more beautiful?"

She stared at him, horrified, and as she stiffened, lifted her hands. They were tied in front of her, and she thought that if she could lift them a bit farther, she should be able to rip the tape off her mouth. Then she could call to Michael.

Michael. Where was he?

He shrugged nonchalantly, almost as if they were just two friends, sharing tea. "So, that's what I did. You can hardly blame me. My stupid father used to drive me up and down this highway when I was a kid, going to horse auctions. He was a rancher, wanted me to be one, too. I didn't want to be one. I wanted to be an artist. Every time I told him that, that I wanted to go to the city for art, I got another fist to the face. So can you blame me for being negative?"

She shook her head to encourage him, a plan solidifying in her mind. Michael probably didn't know this mine shaft was here. It had been hidden from her sight, as well. If she could distract him, she might be able to not only rip the tape off her mouth, but also reach her hands down to her ankles to loosen the tie there. From what she could see, it was only a double knot, and not very tight.

This could work. She took a deep breath, watching him. He was so entranced by his own story that he didn't seem to notice that her eyes were darting elsewhere as she made her plans.

"I appreciate that. Anyway, I was good at math. My mother was a math professor at the University before she married my father and he forced her to quit. She was useless, afraid, refusing to stick up for me, or for her own dreams. We'd drive up and down that highway, completely silent, and I'd count mile posts. Every time I did something wrong, my father would knock my lights out. And the funny thing was, I started noticing-- probably just by coincidence, since my father was too stupid to realize—that all the places where he hurt me corresponded to prime numbers.

"I found it a real hoot. So it wasn't too long before I started instigating him, getting him to punch or slap me on every prime number milepost there was. I remembered every hit, every slap he gave me, based on a number." He smiled. "Seventy-three, I lost two teeth. We'd gotten a flat tire, and I'd done something to provoke him, so he slammed me across the face with a tire iron. I was twelve, and that kept me out of school for two weeks."

His smile grew, and he seemed proud. "So to commemorate my father's actions, I put art there. I find it very healing. I'll replace those bad memories with something beautiful." His eyes glinted, "You."

Her eyes widened in terror. She focused them on the edges of the shaft. Sure enough, she noticed, in the rough walls, some rusted metal footholds. *If I can just get loose of him, I can get out.*

Concern dawned on his face as he looked up toward the opening of the shaft. He twisted his hands together. "Yes. I know, I know, love. It's going to be a little tricky to get you up there. But don't worry." He grabbed a coil of old rope. "Lucky for us, I found this rope up there. It's old, but I think it's pretty sturdy. I'll just tie you up, and I should be able to lift you on out. Sound good?"

He said it as if he was helping her pull her car out of a ditch. Leaning down, he threaded the rope underneath her, tying it in a knot at her belly and giving it a few good tugs.

"That should do it."

Suddenly, a dark shadow fell upon them. For a brief moment, Rylie saw a figure up above.

"Anyone down there?" a voice called.

Michael.

As his full silhouette swallowed up the light in the opening, it plunged them in darkness. Fergus let out a soft growl, stiffening, and whispered, "Make no noise."

She took a deep breath, readying herself.

The second the shadow above moved and the light shone down again, she focused in on her target. His massive, twisted face, leaning toward her.

Banishing the pain screaming through her body, she summoned all her force and shoved upwards, butting him in the face with the top of her head.

He staggered back, moaning. She saw the blood spurting from between his splayed fingers on his face for a split second as she reached her hands up to her face. Despite the screaming pain, she tore the tape off her mouth and called, "Brisbane!"

"You bitch!" he snarled, regaining his balance and reaching for her.

She was folded over, trying to loosen the tie on her ankles. With every bit of force she had left, she lifted both bound hands and drove her closed fists upwards into his jaw. He moaned again and staggered away.

Her hands pressed down into the soft earth as she tried to steady herself. That was when she saw it.

A jagged piece of a broken green beer bottle, half-buried in the dirt.

A shadow loomed overhead, but this time, it wasn't that of a body. Dark clouds shrouded the opening. Weak, vision spinning, she reached down and pulled the final tie that held her ankles together.

He stepped towards her again as thunder rumbled in the distance.

A crooked smile split his face as he came at her, his fists raised above his head, his eyes wide and wild. Her entire body wanted to withdraw, to pull back and seek shelter, but she overruled those desires, clenching her fingers and lunging forward, slashing out with the large, jagged piece of broken bottle in her fists.

Glass cut neatly through tendons as she whipped the jagged glass through Fergus's calf. The sleek and uneven shard slipped through flesh and muscle almost too easily, like a hot knife through butter. It went deep, and the calf split, pulling away from the bone in a vicious spray of red.

This time, Fergus didn't make a sound. He just noiselessly stumbled forward, his leg unable to hold his own weight. Rylie continued forward, keeping low and letting him topple over her. Then she pushed back and spun, lifting the glass up in the air, then plunging it down. Jagged, pointed edges rammed deep into the base of his skull, burying itself into his flesh and spitting out more blood. Warm liquid coated her fingers, and she lost her grip.

"God dammit!" he screamed, throwing a hand on his skull and pulling out the weapon. Staring at in horror, he half-leapt, half-fell on her.

Her head was light and vague as she tried to move into a defensive position. All the muscles of her legs gave out, sending her crashing to the dirt floor. Fergus advanced, his hands raised. She scrambled back, until her back was pressed tight against the rough stone wall, just as the first drops of rain pattered against the dry, dusty ground.

"Stop fighting it, Rylie," he said, somehow managing to stand up straight, despite his injury. He held the bloody piece of glass in front of her. It was his weapon now. "You thought you could make a name for yourself as FBI, right? Save the world, get a plaque in your name. But you can do so much more as a part of my art. You will be known forever as that. Immortalized."

Her eyes stung with the sudden realization of the gravity of the situation. She knew he was insane, but she hadn't known just how far he'd go. That even now, with life-threatening injuries, he'd persist.

He wouldn't stop in his twisted pursuit for this "art" until he was dead.

She eyed the first rung, a rusted metal U. It was within reaching distance, just slightly above his head. It would be hard to climb with her hands bound. Hard, but not impossible. She had to at least try. "Go fuck yourself."

He smiled. It was a sick, sadistic grin, an emotionless, purely superficial gesture. He twiddled his fingers in front of him, and took another step closer. The sight of him bended and twisted in her dizzy vision, and she felt as if she'd soon drop out of consciousness.

Above, thunder slammed and another streak of lighting slashed the sky, pounding the earth, even this far below. It was a sudden, blinding blast of white light, like what she thought the path to heaven might look like.

But this was nothing like that. This was Hell. And he was coming closer, his bloody weapon ready to dig into her flesh.

"How should we do this?" he asked, his voice cracking and slurred with anticipation. "Slow and steady? Quick and painless? I'd think that would be your preference, yes?"

Another step forward, his hands curled around the piece of glass.

Her back was against the wall, figuratively and literally. The rain had picked up, and now it poured relentlessly into her matted, curled hair, running down her face and blurring her vision. But she could not mistake the look in his eyes. It was a narrow and focused realization that her death was imminent. He seemed drunk with that knowledge as he took another confident step towards her.

Without warning, he charged. A guttural snarl exploded from his lips as the jagged weapon cut through air towards her.

Keeping low, she pushed forward with every ounce of her strength, desperate to avoid a fatal slash. The blade slashed in the periphery of her vision as she scrambled away, and crouching, sprang forward into a half desperate leap, her bound hands stretching out, fingers grasping.

She grabbed ahold of the rung and, clinging to it, tried to use her feet to scramble up the side of the wall, toes scraping desperately to find purchase. Despite the wet, slick sides of the wall, she was able to find a foothold. Pushing herself up, she gazed hungrily at the next rung, just a foot or so above her head.

Her wrists burned as she tried to pull them apart, but the rope held fast. If she could move quickly enough, she could reach up and grab the next rung without falling back. Taking a deep breath, she pushed herself up and grabbed, connecting with it and lifting herself up another rung.

Her triumph was short-lived. A second later, he wrapped a hand around her leg and yanked her down. She clung to the wet rung, desperate, until the last second, when the force was too much.

She found herself falling backwards. This time, when she hit the ground, she splashed in thick, viscous mud, sending fireworks of pain up her spine.

She lay there on her stomach, in fetal position, the pain almost too much to bear. Her body flooded with agony. Consciousness ebbed, and her view of the darkened shaft ahead of her blurred into a light fog.

"Time to die," he said.

She agreed.

She felt him splashing toward her as the rain soaked her face, and she felt his presence as he crouched above her, glass at the ready, preparing to land that final, devastating blow.

In those final seconds, she stared death in the face.

She thought of Rose. Of Maren. If it ended here, she'd never know what happened to her sister.

That small thought ignited something in her.

With her last bit of energy, she threw her arms forward. Her face fell in the mud as her fingers curled into fists. Rolling over, bringing her arms up and around, through a vision of fog, her entire body exploding in agony, she swung around and grabbed him, rolling him over into the mud.

She jumped on his back and held him there, pushing him harder into the mud with every lurch his body gave. He gurgled and spit but she held fast to him, shoving his face deeper into the mud, her knees digging into his back until he ceased all movement.

Breathing hard, she pulled herself back and stared at what she had done, emotionless.

When she rolled him over, his eyes were open and empty, that same sick smile upon his face.

"Wolf? Is that you?" Brisbane's voice called overhead.

Rain cascaded on her face. Thunder rumbled in the distance, and a faint gash of lightning lit the sky overhead. Above, she saw her partner's face, eyes wide with worry.

“Where’ve you been, Brisbane?” she called up.

“Oh, God, Wolf. Hold on. I’m coming,” her partner said, and she let out a sigh of relief and fell back against the wall of the cavern.

She closed her eyes and soon fell into a dreamless sleep.

CHAPTER TWENTY NINE

An hour later, Rylie Wolf sat in a hospital bed in the Emergency Room at the Sheridan Medical Center, waving the doctors away. "Really. I'm fine. This is all unnecessary." She pointed at the stupid neck brace that was really cramping her style.

The handsome young doctor stared at her, stone-faced. "I really must insist you get an MRI, at the very least. You probably have a concussion."

She shook her head. "What are you talking about? I'm great," she said, trying to sit up, just to show him how great she was. She tried to throw her legs over the side of the bed and stand up, but her vision did a little dance, and had to reach out for something to steady herself. It wound up being the doctor's shoulder.

He eased her back down. "Now will you get that MRI?"

She averted her eyes. "For what? Even if I do have a concussion, can you do anything for it?"

"You'll need to rest."

She shook her head and tried to cross her arms, but then she remembered her sling. She'd sprained an elbow, but even the sling seemed excessive. Sure, she had bruises all over, and every part of her ached, but she'd get over it. She always did. "I can't do that."

"I don't think you have much of a choice. If you ignore my orders, you can make it worse."

She glowered at him. "But I have to get back on the job. I don't—"

"Is that my partner, going against doctor's advice?" a voice out in the hallway said. "What a surprise."

Brisbane.

He ripped back the curtain and stared at her, shaking his head. "What the hell? I could hear you bellyaching all the way from the parking lot."

She sighed. "I'm not bellyaching. I just don't think there needs to be all this fuss. I'm fine."

"She likely has a concussion. I wanted her to get an MRI," the doctor said, looking down at his tablet. "But she's refusing."

Brisbane fixed her with a disappointed look, as if she were a child who wouldn't finish her vegetables. "What's that all about?"

"I just don't think it's necessary." She waved her free hand. "I don't think any of this is necessary. I'm *fine*. I want to wrap up the investigation and –"

"I can do that," he said.

She shook her head. So she'd nearly gotten killed, and now he was going to swoop in and take credit? No. She didn't care about getting credit, well, not *that* much—she did want to let Matthews and everyone in Seattle know she'd solved the case. But what she did care about, most of all, was that there were still so many loose ends to take care of. "No. I invested a lot of time and effort, and I want to see it through—"

"I know you did, but—"

"So back off," she almost snarled, then immediately felt guilty. She smiled. "Thanks for being out there and rescuing me from that pit. I'd still be there if it wasn't for you."

"Guess partners are good for something," Brisbane's eyes softened, and he looked at the doctor. "Can you give us a moment? I'll try to talk some sense into her."

"You will *not*," she mumbled as the doctor left, pulling the curtain closed behind him.

"Worth a try," he said, the corner of his mouth quirking into a smile. "Look. As your partner, that's what I'm here for. To take up the slack."

"I don't need you to pick up any slack for me. I don't even have slack. I've come this far. I want to see certain things through."

"Like what?"

"Well, what happened to McAdams?"

"Dead," he said, his face solemn. "Turned out he lived in Sheridan all his life. He was always a quiet one, didn't have many friends and family. He'd won a couple of art competitions in the past, but other than that, he'd stayed out of trouble. Something in him must've snapped."

She nodded. "He told me he was abused by his father. He'd always been an artist and his way of stringing those bodies up was creating art, making something he thought was beautiful out of his tragedy." She shuddered at the thought.

"Wow. He was a really sick guy, then, huh?"

She nodded.

"Wow. Anyway, he's responsible for the five murders that we know of. There might be more. But I promise you, that can wait until you've recovered from your injuries."

She shook her head. "That's not all. I wanted to check on McAdams's final victim, and file that final report."

"She's fine," he said, motioning toward the door. "She's in the ICU. Turned out she was pregnant."

"Pregnant? Oh, my God."

"Yeah. But the baby's fine, everything's good. She has a lot of spirit. I'm sure it was traumatizing but she seems to be coping pretty well."

Rylie nodded. She'd hoped that would make her feel a sense of completion, but it didn't. "And the report?"

"I started a draft. I want you to add to it. But don't worry; there's no rush. I filled them in on what happened and they're going to give you as much time as you need to—"

"What did you tell them?" she asked.

"Relax. Nothing bad. I promise, you came out of this looking really good. Like a hero. Everyone's talking about it," he said.

He was trying to appease her.

"It's okay. You can write the report. I'm not that much of a control freak. And I'm sure you didn't make me look bad."

He shrugged. "Yeah, but I have to admit, I'm a little jealous myself. If I'd been the one on the other side of the car, I would've been the one running after McAdams instead of staying with the victim. Then *I'd* look like the hero."

For a flash, it came back to her. That dark hole. The rain. The fight for her life. "Or you'd be—"

"Dead." He nodded. "Most likely, I'd be dead. You did good, Wolf. I'm impressed."

She managed a smile. "Like I said. I couldn't have done it without your help."

He gave her a look that said he wasn't sure. "And yet, you don't want me picking up any slack."

"Okay, maybe I have a *little* slack." She held her fingers up, apart an inch. "You know, I've actually had partners before, but never for very long. I never thought I'd find one that I could work with."

A smile grew on his face. "And that's me?"

"Maybe." She let out a sigh. He'd probably gotten a hint of this, but she felt like she needed to get it out, to clear the air between them. "Truth is, I've been told I'm a little difficult to work with."

He slapped his cheek in mock surprise. "No. Really?"

She nodded, then slapped his shoulder. "I know, right? Hard to believe."

"Anyway," he said, stepping away. "Get that MRI. I promise. All that stuff will be waiting for you when you're ready to tackle it. Okay?"

She nodded, a feeling of relief washing over her. For the first time, she actually trusted her partner would do exactly what he said.

*

The Federal Building, just over the South Dakota border, off the Highway Thru Hell, was a small but distinct building on the outskirts of Rapid City. There was an actual bull standing outside, as if keeping watch over the place, right by the flagpole with the American flag, flapping in the wind.

Her head ached a little as she stood there, staring at the place. The doc was right—she'd had a concussion, so she'd spent a week in the Rapid City apartment they'd set her up in, recovering. Luckily, it was all furnished, so she'd settled in nicely, all the while, dreading today.

This.

Her first "real" day on the job.

Everything before this had felt like just a test, like a precursor to her real work. Though she'd already solved her first case, she hadn't had a chance to visit her new office and meet her new coworkers. This building was perfectly situated in the middle of Highway 86, so it would be proximate to any cases they would put her on.

She stood outside of the building, taking a deep breath, wondering what the day would hold. Meeting new people, trying to make nice . . . she hated it. She hated putting on a front, smiling, trying to get others to like her. She just wanted to go in, get briefed on her next case, and get to work.

When she stepped inside, she headed toward the receptionist, prepared to state her name and ask where she needed to go.

Before she could, someone whistled.

She looked up and saw Michael Brisbane, strolling toward her. "You found the place."

He looked all-too-comfortable in these surroundings. She bet that, unlike her, he loved meeting new people, and had probably become their favorite person, two minutes after arriving. Still, she was relieved to see him. "Yep. You know where my office is?"

"Sure," he said, winking at the receptionist, who gave him a flirtatious, *Hi, Michael!* as he strode toward double doors, his hands in the pockets of his slacks. "All of our unit is over here."

They walked past a cafeteria, and a conference room, and what looked like a library and a storage room. Finally, at a dead end, he pointed to two cubicles, across from one another. "Me," he said, presenting one, and presenting the other, "And you."

She looked around. "Where is everyone else?"

He scratched the side of his head. "They told you the unit's new, right?"

She nodded.

"Well, it's just us. And Bruce Dodd, Special Agent in Charge. His office is over there." He motioned with his chin. "But he's out today. Told me to show you around, make you comfortable."

"So . . . it's just us?"

He nodded, rocking back and forth from his toes to his heels. "Yep. For now. They'll be adding new agents, or so I'm told."

She peered in the cubicle and saw the regular things—a phone, a computer, an office chair. It was pretty bare, except for the several giant banker's boxes of folders that had been in the back of her car. She'd had Michael bring those in, but . . . it seemed that they'd multiplied. There were twice as many as she remembered. "Where did all these boxes come from?"

"The Rapid City Field Office was keeping their own files on crimes."

"These are all the files from the area?"

He shook his head. "Nope. These are all the files that pertain to Highway 86."

Her jaw dropped. It looked like the two of them definitely had their work cut out for them. "Geez. Where do we start?"

He chuckled. "Easy, Bronco. Why don't you start by settling in? Get comfortable. I know HR is going to want to get you set up on email and have your photo taken for your access card."

"Oh. Right."

He knocked on the cubicle wall. "Well, I'll leave you to it. Holler if you need anything."

When he left, she moved some boxes around and set her bag down, then switched on her computer. Sitting down in her office chair, she lifted the lid on a box and pulled out the first file. It was something about a child murder that had taken place, down the highway, in Sioux Falls. The thought was that it could've been related to sex trafficking.

Her thoughts turned to Maren.

Though she'd been young at the time, she'd heard that phrase batted around a lot. Her father had been so distraught, he barely said anything. But all Rylie could think of was her beautiful, vibrant sister, in chains, in a cage, being dragged about and abused, like some animal.

Her stomach roiled at the thought.

Maybe McAdams was right. Maybe it was impossible to eliminate all the bad in the world. But it was worth it to do her part, to eliminate some—even a small part of it. Because evil, like good, was contagious. By stopping one wrong from being committed, who knew how many future crimes she'd prevent? No, it wouldn't make the world perfect, but it would make it better.

And so she would do as much as she could. As she read through file after file, finding more and more shocking crimes, she found herself itching to get back onto the highway and stop as many Fergus McAdams as she could, no matter what the risk.

A moment later, Brisbane appeared in the opening to her cubicle, rubbing his hands together, a wild look in his eyes. "Hey, Wolf. I think I've got something."

"What?" she asked, leaning back, curious. "Like a disease?"

"No, like a case. Something that I think we should be looking into."

Her ears perked up and she wheeled her chair closer to him. "I'm listening."

"You know that trucker who kidnapped that girl a couple weeks ago?" he asked, leaning against the wall of the cubicle. "The one who'd been at the truck stop, with the desert scene on his truck? Clive McDougal?"

She nodded. "Of course. Mac. What's up with him?"

"Well, he's facing life in prison. So in effort to get himself some leniency, he's been talking about all other kinds of crimes he's seen on the route. Turns out he knows some guy who he said admitted to killing a bunch of hitchhikers up in Montana. All young females. And there have been a bunch of missing girls from that area. One named Chrissy Johnson. I remember her name because I saw it in the files."

Her heart quickened. Chrissy Johnson. She recalled that name, too. She'd been bleary, that night in the hotel room, after her long drive from Seattle, but she couldn't forget the girl, because she'd looked like a baby—she'd been only fifteen years old, like poor Ava, Mac's intended victim.

Of course, every one of those girl kidnappings reminded her of Maren, and struck her right in the heart. This would bring her closer to that area where her sister had been taken . . . and with a little digging, who knew what she might find?

"Does he have a name?"

"Part of one. Our trucker friend couldn't stop talking. He has a lot of sketchy details. But I think with his information, and whatever we have in the files, we might be able to make some connections. What do you think? Should we do it?"

She nodded and clapped her hands together. "Hell, yes."

NOW AVAILABLE!

<u>CAUGHT YOU</u>
(A Rylie Wolf FBI Suspense Thriller —Book 2)

On a notorious stretch of highway rife with serial killers, new victims are appearing, their cars crashed off the road by a reckless killer, their bodies missing. What madness drives this serial killer? And can FBI Special Agent Rylie Wolf uncover the pattern and catch him before he disappears for good?

In CAUGHT YOU (A Rylie Wolf FBI Suspense Thriller—Book Two), Rylie, still haunted by a near miss with a murderer during her childhood, tries to avoid facing her past, while hunting down this new killer. When the case leads her down an endless rabbit hole, she's forced to look for answers in unlikely places, even turning to people she hoped to never speak to again.

But she can't open up to her partner about what happened—and the clock is ticking before this killer strikes again.

In a high-stakes game of cat-and-mouse, can Rylie battle her demons and piece together the answers in time?

Or will her demons drive her over the edge?

A complex psychological crime thriller full of twists and turns and packed with heart-pounding suspense, the RYLIE WOLF mystery series will make you fall in love with a brilliant new female protagonist and keep you turning pages late into the night. It is a perfect addition for fans of Robert Dugoni, Rachel Caine, Melinda Leigh or Mary Burton.

Book #3 in the series—SEE YOU—is now also available.

Molly Black

Debut author Molly Black is author of the MAYA GRAY FBI suspense thriller series, comprising six books (and counting); and the RYLIE WOLF FBI suspense thriller series, comprising three books (and counting).

An avid reader and lifelong fan of the mystery and thriller genres, Molly loves to hear from you, so please feel free to visit www.mollyblackauthor.com to learn more and stay in touch.

BOOKS BY MOLLY BLACK

MAYA GRAY MYSTERY SERIES
GIRL ONE: MURDER (Book #1)
GIRL TWO: TAKEN (Book #2)
GIRL THREE: TRAPPED (Book #3)
GIRL FOUR: LURED (Book #4)
GIRL FIVE: BOUND (Book #5)
GIRL SIX: FORSAKEN (Book #6)

RYLIE WOLF FBI SUSPENSE THRILLER
FOUND YOU (Book #1)
CAUGHT YOU (Book #2)
SEE YOU (Book #3)

www.ingramcontent.com/pod-product-compliance
Lightning Source LLC
Chambersburg PA
CBHW030614310726
48979CB00003B/717
* 9 7 8 1 0 9 4 3 9 3 5 6 8 *